From the dark tunnel came the roaring sound of the subway train.

Jostled by the crowd, Rachelle swam against the current, but the tide of humanity pushed her toward the yellow safety boundary painted on the platform floor. Frowning, she held on tight to her purse and tried to shimmy her way through the crowd.

The flat of a hand on her back startled her, and she jerked just as she was shoved hard, causing her to misstep and propelling her to the very edge of the platform. She lost her balance, her arms windmilling.

Terror ripped a desperate scream from her as she plummeted off the platform and onto the tracks.

TRUE BLUE K-9 UNIT:

These police officers fight for justice with the help of their brave canine partners.

Terri Reed's romance and romantic suspense novels have appeared on the *Publishers Weekly* top twenty-five and Nielsen BookScan top one hundred lists, and have been featured in *USA TODAY, Christian Fiction Magazine* and *RT Book Reviews*. Her books have been finalists for the Romance Writers of America RITA® Award and the National Readers' Choice Award, and finalists three times for the American Christian Fiction Writers Carol Award. Contact Terri at terrireed.com or PO Box 19555, Portland, OR 97224.

Books by Terri Reed

Love Inspired Suspense

True Blue K-9 Unit

Seeking the Truth

Military K-9 Unit

Tracking Danger
Mission to Protect

Northern Border Patrol

Danger at the Border
Joint Investigation
Murder Under the Mistletoe
Ransom
Identity Unknown

Buried Mountain Secrets

Visit the Author Profile page at Harlequin.com for more titles.

SEEKING THE TRUTH

TERRI REED

HARLEQUIN® LOVE INSPIRED® SUSPENSE

Special thanks and acknowledgment are given to Terri Reed for her contribution to the True Blue K-9 Unit miniseries.

Recycling programs for this product may not exist in your area.

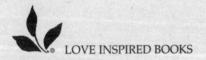

LOVE INSPIRED BOOKS

ISBN-13: 978-1-335-67911-6

Seeking the Truth

Copyright © 2019 by Harlequin Books S.A.

www.Harlequin.com

Printed in U.S.A.

For I know the thoughts that I think toward you, saith the Lord, thoughts of peace, and not of evil, to give you an expected end.
–Jeremiah 29:11

To the men and women of the NYPD who protect
and serve the vibrant city of New York.

To my fellow authors, Lynette, Dana, Laura,
Lenora, Val, Sharon, Shirlee and Maggie—
thank you for your support and patience with me.

To my editors, Emily Rodmell and Tina James—
I so appreciate all you do for me and the books.

And to my faithful friends Leah Vale and Jessie Smith
for reading every word and believing in me.

ONE

The smell of sweaty bodies, garbage from some unseen refuse container and the musty odor of grease from the subway rails lay heavy in the stale August air. Noise bounced off the ceramic tiled walls covered with a dinosaur motif, unique to the 81st Street and Museum of Natural History subway station on the Upper West Side of Manhattan.

The place was crowded due to the Central Park Walkathon. People of all ages and ethnicities mingled on the side platforms. Most wore the green shirts of the walkathon, but there were many other obvious tourists, what with it being late summer, along with local subway passengers.

Officer Carter Jameson kept vigilant for any sort of trouble as he and his K-9 partner, Frosty, an all-white German shepherd, moved from the uptown platform to the downtown platform and back again.

A family of three stepped into his path. The father held an adorable curly-haired toddler in his arms.

"We need to get to the South Street Seaport. Is this the right train?" the mother asked.

"Doggy!" the little girl squealed, her arms reaching out for Frosty. She nearly tumbled out of her father's arms to reach the dog.

The father stepped back, securing his hold on the child. "The dog is working. We can't pet him."

Carter appreciated the father's words. "We are working, but we can take a short break if she'd like to pet him."

He looked down at Frosty and gave the hand gesture to sit, which Frosty immediately obeyed. "Play nice," Carter said, giving the dog the verbal signal that at this moment he was off duty.

Part of Carter's role as an NYC K-9 Command Unit officer assigned to the transit authority was public relations. To let the citizens know they were there to protect and to serve.

"You sure he won't bite?" the man asked, a wary expression on his face.

"Frosty is used to my six-year-old," Carter assured him. "She uses him as a horse."

"That's a cute name for a cute fellow." The mother held out her hand for Frosty to sniff.

Frosty sniffed, then licked her hand, his tail thumping on the hard concrete platform.

"Doggy!" the girl cried again. The father kept her in his arms but squatted down for the child to rub Frosty's coat.

From the pocket of his uniform, Carter withdrew a sticker with the NYPD gold shield and squatted down next to Frosty. Holding out the sticker, he asked the girl, "Would you like to be deputized?"

She clapped her hands.

Peeling the back off the sticker, Carter placed the gold shield on her shoulder. "Now you are one of us."

"Thank you for taking the time with my daughter," the father said as he rose.

The words warmed Carter's heart. He worked hard to uphold not only the code of the NYPD to protect and serve, but also his faith. Not that he and Frosty wouldn't take the bad guys down in a heartbeat, but he'd do so with humility and as much kindness as possible.

Frosty's attention jerked to something behind Carter. The dog didn't alert, but his eyes were fixated on whatever had drawn his focus. Carter could feel a presence hovering.

He glanced over his shoulder. His gaze snagged on a pair of red pumps below well-shaped calves disappearing into a gray pencil skirt.

The reporter?

Two hours ago, his brother Noah, the interim chief of the NYC K-9 Command Unit, had called to warn Carter a reporter wanted to interview him regarding the upcoming national police dog field trials and certification competition, which would be held in two weeks. Carter and Frosty were favored to place high in the public demonstration competition.

A burn of anger simmered in Carter's gut. The way the press had hounded his family the past five months after the unsolved murder of his oldest brother, Jordan, bothered Carter. He had no patience for pushy journalists.

Turning back to the family, he said, "This is the uptown train. The downtown tracks are beneath us. You'll want to get off at Fulton Street. And then walk toward the water. It's easy to find."

"Thank you, Officer," the woman said.

The father held out his hand, which Carter took. "We appreciate your help."

The family turned and walked away.

Carter took a moment for a steadying breath. To Frosty, he murmured, "Work."

The dog's ear perked up, indicating he knew he was back on duty.

"Officer Carter Jameson?"

The honeyed voice, with just a hint of an accent, tripped down his spine.

Unnerved by the visceral reaction, he arranged his features into a neutral expression and turned around. "Yes. May I help you?"

The beautiful woman facing him was tall with long brown hair that floated about her cream-colored, silk-clad shoulders. Brown eyes framed by long lashes stared at him, and her full lips were spread into a tentative smile.

His gaze swept over her. She was dressed to impress, in her fancy blouse and gray pencil skirt. The red pumps were impractical. Though she had on a sturdy-looking cross-body type purse, not so impractical. The flowery notebook and pink pen in her manicured hand would have delighted his daughter, Ellie.

She tucked her pen behind her ear before holding out her hand while gesturing with the notebook to the newsstand that sat in the middle of the platform. "I'm Rachelle Clark with *NYC Weekly*."

He grasped her hand, noting the softness of her skin and the crazy frisson of sensation racing up his arm. "I can't say that I've ever read that particular one."

There were so many local NYC-centric newspapers and magazines keeping those living in the five boroughs up-to-date on the happenings, Carter couldn't possibly read them all.

She extracted her hand. "You don't want to know what's going on in your own community?"

Tucking in his chin, Carter said. "I didn't say that." He narrowed his gaze. "I believe my brother told you I was working."

She had the good grace to grimace. "True." Her smile reappeared. "However, he did tell me where to find you, so I took that to mean he wasn't opposed to me asking you some questions."

"Did he now?" Carter would have to chew Noah out for throwing him to the wolves, or wolf, in this case.

"How about this?" Rachelle said. "I can follow you around the rest of your shift. Just observe. I won't ask any questions." Her accent deepened into a definite Southern drawl. "I won't say anything. Just think of me as a little shadow."

Yeah, right. An attractive shadow. Like having her dogging his steps wouldn't break his concentration. He looked down at Frosty, who looked up at him with his tongue hanging out the side of his mouth.

"We'll take a break right now," he said. "You have five minutes."

"No, no, no. It would do my article so much good if I could see you in action. Even if it's just for a little bit. Then when you're off duty, I can interview you."

Carter rubbed at the tension in the back of his neck. "Like I said, five minutes."

Her gaze darted to his partner then back to him. "He's a handsome dog."

"He knows it," Carter told her.

She laughed slightly but didn't reach out to touch Frosty. Carter wondered if she was afraid or being respectful.

He strode away toward a locked closet built into the staircase, fully aware of his "shadow" following. He tried to ignore the hint of lavender wafting off the woman as he brought out water for Frosty, who lapped it up thirstily. He grabbed his own thermos and drank deeply, his eyes on the reporter watching him.

She glanced around. "Was there a race today?"

"For a reporter, you're not very well-informed." He barely suppressed his amusement when surprise and a bit of annoyance flashed in her chocolate-colored eyes.

She recovered quickly and said through smiling lips, "I don't cover sports."

He couldn't contain the grin tugging at the corners of his mouth. "A walkathon for diabetes. Hardly a sport."

Her eyes narrowed slightly. "Are you expecting trouble?"

Only the kind tall brunettes posed. He shook his head, dislodging that thought. "No. We're just patrolling as a precaution."

"Right." She made a note in that flowery book of hers. "I suppose the walkathon could be a target like last month's Fourth of July celebration."

She was correct, but he didn't comment. No need to give her any more fodder on that score. Two of his fellow K-9 Unit members and their dogs were there when a bomb detonated in a park on the Lower East Side of Manhattan. Thankfully, no one was hurt.

"Did that bombing have anything to do with your eldest brother's murder?"

Carter glanced to her sharply. "Your five minutes is up."

"No, it's not," she countered. She tapped the gold watch on her slender wrist. "I have two more minutes. How close are you to solving your brother's murder case?"

"I thought you wanted to talk about the field trials?"

Her nostrils flared slightly but her smile didn't slip. "I do. Are you and Frosty competing?"

"Yes, we are."

"How many events will you participate in?"

"All of them."

Her dark eyebrows drew together. "Which are…?"

"Obedience and agility. Articles and boxes, which are timed. Apprehension with gun and without gun."

She wrote furiously in her notebook. "Could you elaborate on those?"

"Not now." He tapped her watch. "Time's up. You can attend the public demonstration."

A new flood of people rushed down the stairs toward the train platform. Carter carefully watched the throng and Frosty for any signs of an alert as the dog inhaled the air in short little bursts and sniffed at each person as they walked past him.

It was time to take his focus off the reporter.

Carter put their stash away and closed the closet. "Back to work." He let Frosty lead, his nose twitching in the air.

Awareness shimmied down Carter's spine with every step. He stopped abruptly and turned to face the woman on his heels. Her pumps skidded on the concrete floor, barely halting her in time to keep from bumping into him.

"What are you doing?" he demanded.

Her smile turned saccharine sweet. "There's no law against sharing the same space as you."

Barely refraining from snorting, he blew out a frustrated breath and stalked away.

Rachelle hurried after the handsome police officer and his dog. She'd seen him from a distance at Griffin's Diner, a neighborhood eatery near where she lived in Queens and close to the NYC K-9 Command Unit headquarters, but had never talked to him. Up close the man was downright gorgeous with his dark hair and blue eyes. And fit. She couldn't imagine wearing all the gear attached to his body on a daily basis, let alone in the dank and stuffy subway.

She was glad to see he was thoughtful of his partner to make sure the dog stayed hydrated. She made a note in her journal. She'd always liked dogs from a distance. Her parents had never allowed pets. Which made writing about the K-9 duo that much more fascinating.

It had taken some fancy talking to get her boss to allow her to write an article about the police dog competition because she'd already been assigned to cover an upcoming celebrity ball, which thankfully had some redeeming value as a fund-raiser for autism awareness.

Her hope with the article about the police dog field trials was to gain some insider information on the K-9 Unit and the unsolved murder of NYC K-9 Command Unit Chief Jordan Jameson.

Five months ago when Chief Jameson had failed to appear for a K-9 graduation, the department had known something was wrong. Their chief wouldn't disappear without a word. Then a few days later, Jordan had been found dead in what was made to look like a suicide, but evidence had proven Jordan's untimely death was in fact murder. Someone had killed the man in cold blood and remained at large.

A mystery she wanted to solve in order to be taken seriously as a journalist. If she could shed light on why Chief Jameson was killed, or better yet, solve the case by doing her own investigation...

Her work would be noticed and hopefully picked up by more prestigious media outlets.

She hustled to keep close to Carter and Frosty so she could hear and see what he and the dog were doing as they weaved and bobbed through the swarm waiting for the train. Bodies pressed in around her, the smells of the subway assaulted her senses. Odors she'd yet to get used to, having only been in the city for a year. Her skin itched with the need for fresh air and blue sky. Sweat dampened her blouse, no doubt ruining the fabric. Someone pushed against her, sending her stumbling sideways.

"Hey!" she cried out.

Carter whipped around, his blue eyes meeting hers. She regained her balance, gave him a reassuring nod and headed toward him, dodging a couple of teenagers who were jostling each other.

From the dark tunnel came the roaring sound of the train. People surged forward in anticipation of boarding, each hoping to make it through the doors, in case the train was already full.

Jostled by the crowd, Rachelle swam against the current, but the tide of humanity pushed her toward the yellow safety boundary painted on the platform floor. Frowning, she held on tight to her purse and tried to shimmy her way through the crowd.

The flat of a hand on her back startled her and she jerked just as she was shoved hard, causing her to misstep and propelling her to the very edge of the platform. She lost her balance, her arms windmilling.

Terror ripped a desperate scream from her as she plummeted off the platform and onto the tracks.

A woman's scream punctuated the air, loud gasps from the surrounding crowd following. Horror stole Carter's breath as Rachelle disappeared over the edge of the platform onto the subway tracks.

His heart jumped into his throat, galvanizing

him into action. He pushed through the terrified crowd as he called into Dispatch asking for
backup and for the incoming train to be notified
there was a civilian on the tracks. He prayed the
message would be relayed to the conductor in
time to stop the train short.

Pedestrians yelled and urged Rachelle to get
up. She appeared dazed as she pushed to her
knees. Smears of grease and dirt marred her
skirt and blouse. Shoving back her loose hair,
she lifted her frightened gaze as if looking for
help.

Frosty's frantic barking echoed off the tile
and cement. Agitated, the dog paced the edge
of the platform. Carter held tight to his lead,
afraid the dog would jump onto the tracks to
help save Rachelle.

The train wasn't far down the track. He could
hear the strident squeal of the rails echoing
down the tunnel. There wasn't time for her to
climb back onto the platform.

He didn't think there was even time for her
to run to the other end of the platform where
there was a four-step ladder.

Only one option provided a hope of survival.

He knelt down and cupped his mouth to
shout, "Lie down between the rails."

For a heartbeat, she blinked up at him as if
trying to discern his words.

A gust of wind tore down the tunnel, whipping her hair in front of her face and plastering her skirt to her legs. The approaching train would arrive any second. "Hurry! Lie down. Cover your head!"

In a flurry of movement, Rachelle scrambled to do as directed. She lay prone between the inside tracks, her face tucked into the crook of her elbow.

Even if the train didn't hit her, there was no guarantee the equipment hanging down from the undercarriage wouldn't cause injury.

Nausea roiled through his gut as he pushed to his feet and lifted a prayer for this woman's safety. "Please, God."

Rachelle squeezed her eyes tight. Her heart hammered in her chest. She covered her head with her purse, thankful it hadn't flown off her body in the fall, and fought to lie as still and flat as possible.

If she survived this…

No! She would survive this—she'd be headline news. And could write about the fast-thinking officer who helped her stay alive.

The loud squeal of the rails shuddered through her. Her body tensed.

"Please, Lord. Please, Lord." She repeated the refrain over and over.

* * *

The sight of the incoming train filled Carter with terror. He waved his arms over his head, hoping to grab the train engineer's attention. Others joined in.

The sound of people crying mixed with the screech of the brakes as the train decelerated and came to a jerking halt within inches of Rachelle's feet.

A cheer broke out.

Sweat soaked Carter's back beneath his uniform and flak vest. "Thank you, Jesus."

To Frosty, he commanded, "Stay."

He dropped the dog's lead and then jumped down onto the tracks, careful to avoid the third rail, which supplied live electrical power for the subway to run efficiently. It was exposed and extremely dangerous. He hurried to gather Rachelle into his arms and lifted her off the ground. Her arms encircled his neck and she buried her face in his shoulder. Her body trembled. Shock, no doubt.

"You're okay," he assured her.

He carried her to the end of the platform. Several people rushed to help her up the stairs.

"My notebook and pen!"

Carter rolled his eyes at her priorities but quickly grabbed her items before climbing up the ladder behind her.

Rachelle's pretty brown eyes were wide, the pupils dilated. She wobbled on her pumps and gripped his arm. "Thank you. That was really close."

Tell me about it. "You're going to be okay."

He slid an arm around her waist and led her to the bench against the wall. He squatted down beside her, setting her notebook and pen on the bench.

Frosty put his chin on her knee. She stroked the dog behind the ears with one hand and placed her other hand protectively over her notebook.

"What happened?" Carter asked.

Her lips trembled. "Someone pushed me."

Shock reverberated through him. The platform was now a crime scene. He radioed in this new development.

"That's right. I saw the whole thing." An older gentleman stepped forward. "Guy wore a gray T-shirt, baseball hat and sunglasses. He had brown hair, medium height."

Carter rose and searched the pressing crowd. "Can you point him out?"

"As soon as he pushed her, the guy ran up the stairs," the older man told him. "I heard him say, 'You're getting too close.'"

"I heard him say that, too." A young woman

wearing a walkathon T-shirt stepped forward. "I saw him put his hand on her back and push."

Carter's gaze snapped back to Rachelle. "Why would someone want to hurt you?"

She tucked in her chin. "You think I was targeted?" Something flashed in her eyes, some thought that made her frown, but then she shook her head. "No. It was crowded. He probably got claustrophobic. It had to have been a random act."

Carter wasn't sure what to think. He didn't have time to question her further as other police officers and paramedics flooded the platform. He greeted the officers, explained the situation and let them interview the witnesses. Carter would write up his statement when he returned to his home station in Queens.

The medical personnel fussed over Rachelle. She waved them away. "I'm fine. Nothing is broken. Nothing's twisted. I'll have some bruises, but you can't help with that."

Carter touched her shoulder. He'd already noted the scrapes on her hands and the smudges on her knees. She'd dropped four feet onto hard concrete. "Let them do their jobs."

She huffed out a sigh and tucked her notebook and pen into her purse. "I've taken worse falls. My parents have a grand oak that rises a hundred feet in the air. I've fallen out of it more times than I can count. This was barely a tumble."

Her words were saying one thing, but her body was shaking beneath his hand. "Humor me."

Her lips pressed together, and she nodded. The EMTs checked her vitals, assessed her limbs for injury. They declared her okay but told her to rest and put ice on her knees.

When the paramedics retreated, she rose from the bench, straightened her dirt-smudged skirt and squared her shoulders. Looking him in the eye, she said, "What I would like to do is interview those witnesses, then get on with our interview."

She had gumption, he'd give her that. He admired that she wasn't rushing out of the subway system scared as a rabbit. Most people would be anxious to escape the area after experiencing something as traumatic as being pushed into the path of a subway train.

Who had pushed her? And why?

Random? Or a targeted attempt on her life?

TWO

"We're heading back to our unit's headquarters in Queens," Carter said to Rachelle as he reined her in from questioning the witnesses.

He was determined to discover the truth about why someone would want to harm her, which meant he needed to keep her close and grill her about the incident. "Come along with us."

"Wonderful. I live not far from there. Do you think I could get a tour of the station?"

"I'm sure that can be arranged." Carter looked down at Frosty, who stared at him with trusting eyes. "All right, partner, let's head out."

The dog's ears perked up, his tail thumped once and then he stood. The crowd had thankfully thinned. Yet, Carter couldn't shake the stress of seeing Rachelle tumbling off the platform onto the tracks.

"Let's go aboveground where we can hail a taxi."

"You don't have a vehicle?"

"I do, but parking in the city is nearly impossible for any length of time."

"Would you normally travel back to Queens via a cab?" she asked, her intelligent eyes studying him.

"No. Part of our job with the transit bureau is to ride the subway," he told her. "But we can take a cab today."

She shook her head. "Not on my account. I'd rather you do as you normally would. It would be better for my story."

Grudgingly, he respected her dedication. He shrugged. "Suit yourself."

They walked to the platform for the downtown train and stood behind the yellow painted barrier.

He doubted Rachelle realized he'd slowed his pace to keep her within reach so he could grab her and protect her at the first sign of danger. Coming from a family with a long line of police officers, protecting others was built into his DNA.

His cell phone rang. The caller ID announced his brother Noah. Again. Two calls in one shift? Carter quelled the spike in his pulse. Noah had offered to watch Carter's daughter, Ellie, on his day off because their parents were unavailable.

Keeping an alert eye on those around them, he pressed the button. "Hey, just about to leave the city. Your reporter friend has asked for a tour of the station." Carter glanced at Rachelle, watching her scribble in her flowered notebook.

Noah chuckled. "Not my friend, pal. But I'm glad you're not complaining."

"That will happen later. It's been exciting so far." *Traumatic* would be a better descriptor but Carter would save the story for when he saw Noah.

"Well, you can start complaining now. I've been called into headquarters. My day off is over, and my babysitting time is up."

Hope flared. "News on Jordy's killer?"

Rachelle's gaze snapped to his. Carter saw the curious gleam in her eyes. *Reporter, remember!* He couldn't let his guard down around her. He'd learned the hard way the media only wanted the sensational and twisted the truth to meet their own narrative.

Noah sighed. "No. Nothing to do with the case."

Disappointment curdled the hope.

"You'll need to come directly home," Noah continued. "Mom and Pop aren't back from Fire Island yet."

"Is Zach around?" Even though his youngest brother had married and moved out, he came around the family home often. His brothers took turns babysitting Carter's six-year-old when their mom and dad were not available.

"On patrol this evening. And Katie's not feeling well."

Katie, Jordan's widow, was five months pregnant. Carter's heart ached knowing his oldest sibling would never get to hold his child, watch his child take his or her first steps, or hear the sweet voice of his own kid calling him Daddy.

Carter cleared his throat before he could speak. "Why don't you bring the munchkin to the station house. I'll grab her there."

"Will do." Noah hung up.

Rachelle raised an eyebrow. "Everything okay?"

"Yes." He was saved from having to explain further by the arrival of the train. "Here we go."

They boarded a middle car. As usual, he and Frosty were greeted with a mix of nervous glances and stiffened spines or open interest. Carter gestured for Rachelle to take a seat near the car's end door. He and Frosty stood guard.

Until he was satisfied that the attempt on Rachelle's life had truly been a random act of violence, he planned to unearth all he could about the pretty reporter and what she might be working on that would put her life in danger.

Rachelle kept her gaze on Carter as the subway train zoomed down the track. The rhythmic noise of the rails brought back the memory of the train bearing down on her. A shudder ripped through her, setting off a maelstrom of pain from the many bumps and bruises the fall caused. She forced the horrific images of what had happened earlier away. However, the fear lingered. She'd probably have nightmares tonight.

Or dreams of strong arms, making her feel safe and secure, lifting her from the train tracks while the thunderous applause from the crowd and the bark of the world's cutest dog rang in her ears.

She pushed the thought aside, too. It was fine she found Carter good-looking and she was grateful for his rescue, but she wasn't looking for anything more from him than a source that would provide her a front-page story to bring justice to the world.

Or, at least, justice for his brother.

And earn her notice from prestigious news outlets.

Consciously redirecting her mind to the phone call Carter had received, curiosity burned through her veins like a wildfire. She wanted to know more about Chief Jordan Jameson's murder. But the look of disappointment on Carter's face had let her know the call hadn't been about the investigation. "Who's 'the munchkin'?"

Carter folded his arms over his chest. "My daughter."

Ah. A call from the wife. Why would he be

asking his spouse about Jordan's murder? "Is your wife in law enforcement, also?"

His jaw hardened. He kept his gaze forward this time. Not even looking at her. His Adam's apple bobbed. For a long moment he stayed silent, his expression unreadable and she feared she'd just overstepped with her question.

"I'm a widower." His voice came at her low and sharp.

Her heart clenched. Had his wife died in the line of duty? An innocent bystander? Or an illness? Or some other horrible death? It was too much to bear thinking about. She went back to her earlier question. Munchkin was his daughter. "How old is she? Your daughter," she clarified.

"Six."

"That must be hard. Raising a child on your own. How old was she when her mother passed?"

He shifted his stance, tucking his hands behind his back and widening his feet. "These are not questions I choose to answer in this venue."

Properly chastised, she folded her hands over her notebook in her lap. Yes, this wasn't the place to ask about his personal life. Too many ears, too many eyes and too many unknowns. "Of course. Forgive me."

He remained silent, but his chin dipped slightly. Rachelle would take the slight movement as forgiveness from a guy like Officer Carter Jameson any day of the week.

She glanced warily around the subway car. Several people were clearly nervous to have an officer and K-9 on board. It was a diverse group of individuals. Some were clearly families heading home from a day in the city. Others obviously were tourists, with cameras around their necks or holding subway maps in their hands. The rest of the passengers most likely were workers getting off from their city jobs, possibly heading home to one of the other boroughs where it wasn't so expensive to live.

She found herself looking for a man in a gray T-shirt and baseball hat with brown hair, of medium height. None fit that description in the car. Could the incident on the subway platform have been related to her investigation into Jordan Jameson's murder? She suppressed a shiver of dread.

A casual glance at Carter found him watching her with his inscrutable gaze. Unperturbed, she met his gaze fully and assessed him as he assessed her. This was a man who was used to intimidating others. With nothing more than a stony stare, a formidable stance and a big dog.

She'd learned a lot in the last year since moving to New York City. Who to stay away from, who might cause trouble and that at any moment some celebrity, thinking they were incognito, could appear right next to her on a subway car, a street corner or in a restaurant. Carter wouldn't be looking for celebrities. He'd be looking for the ones who were doing bad things.

Like the guy who'd pushed her off the platform. She knew to keep her eyes open and sharp. The fact that she'd failed to notice the danger really irked her. She should never have allowed herself to get close enough to the edge to be pushed off. Normally, she stayed back until the train came to a stop. The only explanation had to be she'd been too focused on Carter.

When the subway train pulled into the next station, Carter and Frosty moved to stand near the opening doors. The dog sat at Carter's heels, his nose twitching at everyone who came in and out of the car.

"How did you come up with the name Frosty?" she asked him.

Carter glanced over his shoulder at her and arched an eyebrow.

Raising her hands in acknowledgment that she'd received the message—*not here, not now*—she opened her notebook and added more questions to her growing list. She kept her mouth closed for the remainder of the ride but couldn't help the impatient bounce of her foot as the subway car rolled along.

She was glad when they finally switched trains to head out of Manhattan to the borough of Queens.

As they exited the subway car, Rachelle was sure she heard several sighs of relief. She didn't understand why the dog and officer made people so anxious. Carter and Frosty were there to serve and protect. Yes, the police in general seemed to have a bad rap in the media over the last few years. And she wasn't naive—she knew there could be bad apples on any tree. But the NYC K-9 Command Unit had, until recently, a really good reputation.

However, people were losing confidence that the K-9 Unit could solve their own chief's murder, let alone any other crime. After five months with no answers, she had to admit she was frustrated, too. Which in part was what had prompted her to begin her own investigation.

Along with the fact she wanted to advance her own career.

But she'd rather think about the more altruistic reason she was diving headlong into Jordan Jameson's life. His murderer needed to be caught and justice served. She and everyone else in New York would sleep better knowing a killer was off the streets.

A shiver traipsed down her spine, reminding her of the terrifying event she suffered in the subway. She rubbed at the dirt streaked across her skirt. The skin underneath protested. In fact, her whole body ached from the impact of the fall now that the shock had eased.

She really didn't want to contemplate why someone had pushed her off the subway platform. Better to chalk it up to a onetime thing than to live in fear. She refused to believe the incident had anything to do with her inquiries into Jordan's life.

With Frosty on Carter's left and Rachelle on his right, they walked away from the subway station and onto the sidewalk. This was her neighborhood. The residual fear and stress keeping her muscles bunched tight throughout her body began to melt away like butter on her grandma's biscuits. They neared the mini market where a slim man in his sixties swept the front walkway.

"Good afternoon, Mr. Lee," she called with a wave.

Mr. Lee looked up and smiled at her. "Ah, Miss Rachelle." His gaze narrowed at Carter and Frosty. "Are you okay?"

"Perfect," she replied. "You?"

"Well, thank you." He hurried inside the store.

They headed down the street with the late afternoon traffic buzzing by. She could feel Carter's curious gaze. She glanced at him sideways. "My apartment is only a few blocks from here. I stop in occasionally for fruit or milk." Her own curiosity prompted her to ask, "Do you two always receive that sort of reaction? I noticed on the subway that many people were nervous with you two aboard."

He shrugged. "It happens. Some people get antsy around authority figures. We're trained to discern the difference between a nervous Nellie and a real crook." He peered at her. "How did you end up in New York?"

"Who doesn't want to live in New York?" She wasn't about to tell him she had applied and accepted the job at *NYC Weekly* as a way to escape her family. "My hope is to write something that will be picked up by a major news source and lead to a job with them. And this New York job seems the best possible place for that to happen."

"Why journalism?"

She shrugged. "When it was time for college, my maternal grandmother suggested journalism." She affected a prim voice. "'Turn your rebelliousness to usefulness,' was her advice. I took it."

"She sounds like a wise woman."

Sadness slipped over her. "She was. She passed on while I was in college."

"I'm sure she would have been proud of you," he commented.

At the corner, they waited for the light to turn green before crossing.

"Thank you for saying so." She didn't add that her father had said the opposite when she'd made the decision to leave Georgia.

The walk signal appeared, and she stepped out onto the street.

The squeal of tires on the hot pavement filled the air. A car careened around the corner, aiming straight at her. Her lungs froze. Her body refused to move. Carter's hand wrapped around her biceps and yanked her back onto the sidewalk mere seconds before the brown sedan whizzed past, barely missing her.

She put a hand over her beating heart. "Crazy driver."

Carter regarded her with an intensity that set the fine hairs on her nape to high alert. He used the radio on his shoulder to report the incident and the fact the car's license plate had been removed.

"Come on." He ushered her quickly across the street to a three-story brick building with square windows and an American flag waving over the entrance. Carter stopped to open the glass doors of the public entrance.

"Would there be time for a tour?" She didn't

like the way her voice quaked. The fright from nearly being run over still zoomed through her veins. Having her life flash before her eyes twice in one day made her nerves raw.

Carter's mouth lifted at one corner. "Yes, I'm sure that can be arranged."

Excited by the prospect of seeing the inner sanctuary of the K-9 Unit, she followed him inside. Carter and Frosty patiently waited while she went through security and then received a visitor's badge from the front desk officer sitting behind a large U-shaped desk.

Having never been inside a New York Police Department precinct, she found it fascinating. The lobby had a warmth to it she hadn't expected. Pictures of dogs and their handlers gave the beige walls life. The phones rang incessantly, keeping the receptionist busy.

Joining Carter and Frosty near a set of stairs, she observed, "Much different than the small police station back home."

Carter led her up a flight of stairs. "Really? Where is back home and why do you know what the inside of the police station looks like?"

"Vidalia, Georgia. As to why…" A flush heated her cheeks. "I was a bit of a rebellious scamp as a child. I was caught picking flowers in Mrs. Finch's garden. My father thought he'd scare some sense into me by dragging me down to the sheriff's station and demanding that Sheriff Potter put me in jail. I think he wanted to frighten me straight as it were."

Pausing, Carter stared at her. "Seriously? The sheriff didn't…"

"No. He told me to apologize to Mrs. Finch and he never wanted to see me inside the station house again. He never did."

"Hmm."

She wasn't sure she wanted to know what he was *hmm*ing about.

They entered a large space dotted with cubicles for the officers and their dogs. At the far end were enclosed offices. Carter led her to his desk, where he locked his weapon in the bottom drawer. Frosty lay down on a large round fluffy bed underneath the desk corner.

"Can you tell me now how Frosty got his name?"

Carter hitched a hip on the edge of his desk. "He's named after William Frost. He was an officer with the NYPD back in the '80s. He was murdered in a gang-related shooting."

A pang of sorrow touched her. "That's so sad. Do all the dogs get their names from fallen officers?"

"They do, in some variation. I chose Frost rather than William because he was all white like a blast of winter frost."

"What breed is he?"

"German shepherd."

"Really? I've never seen one like him before."

"The white version of the breed comes out of Canada."

"That's funny. The Great White North." She wrote that down. "You said Frost, but you call him Frosty."

"Ellie, my daughter, liked Frosty better. And it stuck."

"What a pretty name. Ellie. Your daughter sounds charming."

"She is." He looked past her, and his features visibly changed, taking on a soft tender look that had her heart thumping against her rib cage.

She turned to see a blond-haired, blue-eyed pixie streaking toward them.

The little girl jumped into her father's arms. "Daddy!" she squealed.

She gave Carter big, noisy kisses on both cheeks.

Carter's deep rumble of a laugh hit Rachelle like an acorn from her parents' oak tree, digging into her psyche and making her want to hear more.

Holding his beautiful little girl on his hip, Carter smiled at Rachelle. "This is Ellie." The child regarded her with open curiosity. "My pride and joy."

There was no doubt about that. "Hi, Ellie, it's nice to meet you."

"Honey," Carter addressed his daughter, "this is Ms. Clark. She's a reporter."

The way he emphasized the word *reporter* had Rachelle stiffening her spine. Wariness entered the little girl's shining eyes. "She's one of those."

Rachelle tried not to take offense. Clearly the Jamesons didn't hold reporters in high regard.

"All right, you two," a deep masculine voice from behind Rachelle admonished. "No need to scare our guest."

Rachelle spun around to find herself face-to-face with Chief Noah Jameson. She'd seen his picture in the *New York Times*, as well as her own paper on numerous occasions over the past several months.

Dark circles were evident beneath his green eyes. She could only imagine the stress of losing one brother and taking over a high-profile position amid controversy.

Rachelle scribbled down her observations, her pink pen flying over the pages of her flowered journal.

"I like your book," Ellie said. "Can I see it?"

Rachelle clutched the notebook to her chest and gave a nervous laugh. "These are my work notes. I'm doing an article on your father. And Frosty."

Carter set Ellie's feet on the floor. "Okay, munchkin, I need a moment with Uncle Noah."

He glanced at Rachelle. "I need to tell Noah about today. All of it."

Rachelle swallowed back the sudden jump of residual fear. "We'll be fine here."

She looked at Ellie and was a bit disconcerted by the way the girl was assessing her, much as her father had done.

As the two men walked away Ellie asked, "What happened to your skirt? It's dirty."

Smoothing a hand over the mark, she replied, "I fell." She didn't add she'd been nearly run down in the street. And almost flattened by a train.

Ellie slipped her hand into Rachelle's. "Is my daddy helping you?"

Carter certainly had his hands full with this little perceptive child. "Yes. Yes, he is."

And she couldn't begin to express her gratitude to him for not only saving her life but also for being a path to furthering her career.

"Are you married?"

Taken aback by the little girl's question, Rachelle glanced up to see Carter had paused midstep as if he'd heard his daughter's query. His lips twisted in a rueful grimace before he turned and walked into Noah's office, closing the door behind him.

Smothering a grin, Rachelle shook her head at the little girl. "No, I'm not." And she had no plans to be for the foreseeable future.

Ellie's eyes lit up. "That's good."

Deciding it was best not to pursue that comment, Rachelle asked, "School must be starting soon, right?"

The little girl released Rachelle's hand and hopped onto her father's desk chair. With the heel of her hand on the desk, she sent the chair spinning. "Yep. In a couple weeks. I'm not looking forward to it."

"Why not?"

Ellie stopped spinning and stared at her. "It's school."

As if that should explain everything. Rachelle laughed. "Well, there is that. But aren't you excited to see all your friends and have recess and art? Art was always my favorite subject. I could get messy and not get in trouble." Though with budget cuts she wasn't sure art was taught anymore in public schools.

Ellie resumed her spinning. "Oh yes. I'm excited to see Kelly and Greta. I'll be in Mrs. Lenny's class. We'll get to do a garden project. My daddy said I could bring butterflies."

"He did, did he? That's fabulous. You have a good daddy."

"Yep." Ellie stopped the chair to peer at her. "He'd be a good catch, as my grandma says."

Uh-oh. Was she trying to play matchmaker?

THREE

Not going to happen. What to say that wouldn't offend or be rude? Rachelle settled for, "Interesting."

Ignoring Ellie's assessing gaze, Rachelle busied herself visually memorizing everything on Carter's desk. Everything in its place. Pens and pencils corralled in an NYPD mug. Reports stacked with clean edges on one side of the desktop while a dormant computer screen and keyboard took up the other half. No dust bunnies, either.

A family photo of the Jamesons sitting next to the computer caught her attention. Recently taken, by the looks of it. Carter and Ellie, much as the little girl appeared now, were crouched down in the front row, while Carter's three brothers, including the murdered Jordan, stood behind them. Snuggled up to Jordan was a pretty blonde woman. No doubt Jordan's widow, Katie.

Next to the Jameson family photo sat a gilded

framed wedding photo of a young-looking Carter standing with his radiant bride. Ellie got her blond hair and delicate features from her mother.

A pang tugged at Rachelle's heart. No wonder Carter wanted Ellie to have butterflies in her life. They represented renewal and hope. "You can't have a garden without butterflies."

Ellie pushed off the desk and sent the chair whirling in a circle. "I have some carrot seeds that Aunt Katie got for me."

"That was nice of her."

"She said I should contribute to the vegetables, too."

A big word for a little girl. No doubt she was repeating what she'd heard. "Katie's a smart woman. Do you see her often?"

Ellie stopped spinning again. The corners of her sweet little mouth pinched inward. "She lives with us. She's very sad because Uncle Jordy went to Heaven."

Heart aching for this family's loss, Rachelle said, gently, "That's totally understandable. I'm sure you're sad, too."

The girl's eyes misted. She nodded. "I miss Uncle Jordy. He gave the best tickles. My daddy is sad, too. He misses Uncle Jordy and…because my mommy went to Heaven." Ellie's gaze was on the wedding photo.

Rachelle blinked to repel the sudden moisture gathering in her own eyes. "Do you remember her?"

Ellie shook her head. "No. Mommy died right after I was born."

Flooded with sympathy for this young little girl and her father, Rachelle didn't quite know what else to say. What could she say? The little girl had experienced more heartbreak than most people in her short time on earth. "So, does Frosty live with you guys?"

Ellie sent the chair spinning once more. "He sure does. Also Scotty—he's Uncle Noah's dog—and Eddie, Uncle Zach's dog. But Uncle Zach and Eddie moved out." Her little brow furrowed. "Snapper lived downstairs with Aunt Katie and Uncle Jordan, but we don't know where he is right now."

Rachelle remembered the name from the news reports. Snapper was Chief Jordan Jameson's missing dog.

"Now Mutt and Jeff live with us, too." Ellie giggled. "Those aren't their real names. That's just what Dad calls them."

"Your uncles?"

"No, silly." Ellie waved a hand in a swatting motion. "The puppies. They are both girls, but Daddy still calls them by boy names. They are with us to be—" She paused and appeared to concentrate as she said, "Socialized." She grinned. "But they're gonna be police dogs just like Frosty and Scotty. Frosty's not too fond of them. They get on his nerves. He growls, but they don't care. They just run right on top of him. Scotty's better with them. He just walks away when they bug him."

"Sounds entertaining." She would like to see the dogs and puppies together. Rachelle glanced at one dog in question. Frosty looked so peaceful lying there with his snout on top of his crossed paws. He opened one eye as if he sensed her attention.

Awareness cascaded over her flesh and she turned to find Carter approaching. The man exuded vitality even from five feet away. She mentally shook off the odd sensation.

"Ellie, sweetie," Carter said. "Can you hang with Frosty for a moment while I show Rachelle something?"

"Yes, Daddy." Ellie crawled off the chair and flopped down on the round bed on the floor, practically lying on top of the dog. Frosty's ears twitched, his tail thumped, but otherwise he made no move.

Amazed at how calm and loving the dog was with Ellie, Rachelle asked, "Are you sure he's a police dog?"

"He can be fierce when he needs to be," Carter told her.

She wasn't sure she believed his assurance. "If you say so."

"He has a really good track record of taking down criminals. He's a multipurpose trained dog. Part of our job with the transit bureau is public relations."

"Like with the little girl and her father today." Rachelle had been surprised to see the child petting the working dog when she'd approached Carter.

"Exactly." He cupped her elbow. "Come with me."

She sucked in a breath at the unexpected contact but forced herself to focus on the excitement of being given a glimpse of the rest of the precinct. Anticipating a tour of the facility, she was surprised by their first stop. He led her into a room filled with video monitors. A curvy female officer with long, curly blond hair tied back with a rubber band sat reviewing the screens. The woman turned to regard them with hazel eyes behind huge framed glasses. "Hey, Carter. What's going on?" Her gaze raked over Rachelle.

Uncomfortable beneath the other woman's curiosity, Rachelle fought the urge to fiddle with her purse strap or fix her hair. Best never to let anyone see a weakness. She lifted her chin, met her gaze and smiled.

"Hi, Danielle," Carter said. "This is Rachelle Clark. Rachelle, Danielle Abbott, our computer tech."

"Nice to meet you," Rachelle said, then winced inwardly at how her accent had thickened. It did that sometimes when she was nervous.

"Likewise." Danielle's curiosity sparkled in her hazel eyes.

"I need a favor," Carter said.

"Sure." Danielle's gaze snapped back to Carter. "Anything."

"Can you access the MTA database and bring up the video surveillance from the 81st and Museum of Natural History subway platform?"

"Of course. We have access to all the five boroughs' databases."

As Danielle's fingers flew on the keyboard, Carter told her the time frame he needed to review.

Rachelle's heart rate ticked up as she realized he wanted to see the push that had caused her fall. Steeling herself against reliving the nightmare, she hovered over Carter's shoulder.

"Here you go," Danielle said.

"Fast-forward a bit," Carter instructed.

It was strange to watch people in the video

coming and going at a fast clip. There was the family she'd found Carter talking to when she arrived. Then she was on-screen talking to him. She couldn't help but critique herself. She hadn't realized she'd fidgeted with her notebook and pen the whole time she'd been talking to him. A nervous habit. One she intended to break.

"There!" Carter pointed to the screen.

Coming down the stairs was a man wearing jeans, a gray T-shirt, baseball cap and sunglasses. He stepped onto the platform and wandered from one end to the other, slowly making his way closer and closer to Rachelle with each pass.

Everyone surged forward in anticipation of the train's arrival.

The mystery man paused right behind Rachelle. From the angle of the video it was too hard to see his hand on her back, but then she was stumbling, her feet trying to find purchase on the slick floor. The man watched her go over the edge of the platform, and then he turned and fled back up the stairs just as the witnesses had said. The video screen froze.

A shudder of terror worked its way over Rachelle's limbs. She wrapped her arms around her middle. Definitely nightmares tonight.

Danielle turned to face her with wide eyes. "That was you."

Rachelle nodded, feeling a bit sick to her stomach.

"There's no good shot of his face. He obviously knew where the cameras were located." Frustration reverberated in Carter's voice.

Finding her own voice, Rachelle stated, "That still doesn't mean it was a deliberate act. He probably didn't realize how hard he pushed me, then got scared when I fell. He doesn't look familiar to me."

Carter frowned. "How would you even know if he was familiar to you? He was never directly in front of you, so you never got a good look at him."

She couldn't argue with his logic. She shrugged, hoping the fear stealing over her wasn't apparent. If this was a targeted incident…

"Danielle, I need to see what cameras we have on the street between here and the subway."

Without a word, the tech analyst swung back around to her monitors and typed on her keyboard. A few seconds later, traffic cameras from the area appeared.

"Go back about half an hour," Carter said.

The video was a blur in Rewind but then came into sharp focus as Rachelle and Carter stepped into view to wait for the light to change at the corner. As the video rolled forward it caught Carter rescuing her from the careening sedan.

"I thought so," Carter muttered.

"What?" Rachelle asked, unsure what he'd seen.

To Danielle he asked, "Can you pull video from the street right outside of the subway station about ten minutes prior to when the sedan showed up there?"

When the video was running, Carter pointed to the sedan parked at the curb. It pulled away and slowly rolled down the street.

"The sedan was waiting. Whoever it is knows where you live and expected you to take the train home." His grim gaze met hers. "It deliberately tried to hit you."

"And the plates were pulled," Danielle mused, sending Carter a look even a noncop could decipher.

Rachelle swallowed back the bile rising in her throat. Her mind went numb. Someone was trying to kill her?

"Thank you, Danielle," Carter said as he put his hand on the small of Rachelle's back and led her out of the video monitoring room.

In the hallway, he stopped her. "Now we know. You're being targeted. Why?"

Hoping to buy time to make sense of things,

she bristled. "Why are you making this out to be my fault?"

"I'm not saying it's your fault." He frowned. "I'm just wondering what kind of stories you've been working on that would generate somebody's animosity."

Someone like the person who killed Jordan Jameson?

She leaned against the wall as her knees weakened. "My assignments are fluff pieces," she told him, which was the truth. "In fact, I'll be covering the upcoming celebrity charity ball at The Met next week. I had to talk my editor into giving me a shot at writing an article about the K-9 trials. He wanted to give it to one of the boys."

"Boys?"

"The male staffers," she clarified, "though they usually act like teenage boys."

"Would one of them have a reason to want to harm you?"

She let out a grim laugh. "No. The guys are harmless. Macho, arrogant, egotistical, but harmless."

He peered at her closely. "What aren't you telling me?"

How did he know?

It could only be one thing that had put her in the crosshairs of a killer, but if she told Carter about her investigation into his brother's death then any hope of advancing her career by solving Jordan Jameson's murder would be gone.

But if she died, then what did her career matter?

Carter watched the play of emotions on Rachelle's pretty face. He wanted her to trust him but wasn't sure how to make that happen. They'd only just met. Trust had to be earned. But he'd saved her life twice. Such heroics had to go a long way toward building confidence in his ability to protect her. "Whatever it is, spit it out. I can help you."

The noise she made was half moan, half scoff. "I think I know what the guy who pushed me meant by 'You're getting too close.'"

"Go on. Tell me."

She licked her lips. His eyes tracked the motion.

"I am working on an investigative piece."

He jerked his gaze from her mouth to her eyes. "Into what?"

Inhaling as if to brace herself, she breathed out and said, "Your brother's death."

"Excuse me?" He reeled back a step, his mind grasping to comprehend her words. "You're... I thought you said you're only assigned fluff pieces."

"I am. This is something I'm doing on my own."

His fingers curled. "You're investigating Jordan's murder. Unbelievable." He hadn't been prepared for that. But she was a reporter, after all. He should know better than to think she would be different than the vultures who'd circled for weeks after Jordan's death. "You're interfering in a police investigation. Do you know how much trouble you're in?"

Her chocolate-brown eyes implored him to understand. "I'm seeking the truth. And there's no way I'm impeding the NYPD's investigation. But obviously I've struck a nerve somewhere."

Anger put an edge to his voice. "Yes. Digging into things you have no business digging into can do that."

She held up her hands. "Hey, all I've done is look up public records, searched social media, made a few dozen phone calls asking people for information. Information they might not be as willing to tell the police. Like the rumors of nepotism and favoritism."

He tucked in his chin. "What are you talking about?"

The look she affected was one of *are you kidding*. "It's a bit strange, don't you think, the way Jordan rose through the rank and file so quickly? Your grandfather was with the NYPD, correct? Your father, too."

Drawing up to his full height of six feet, he

stared at her. "Really? Lady, you don't know what you're talking about. Jordan excelled at his job. He rose to the top by hard work and grit. Just like Noah has."

"Okay, I'm only repeating what I've heard." Her gaze bored into his. "And then there's Jordan and Katie's whirlwind romance. They went from dating to marriage to baby super fast."

Stunned by her audacity, he could barely form words. "You have no right to invade our lives without permission. Katie and Jordan live...led—" the grief he kept under a tight leash bubbled to the surface, breaking his voice "—squeaky-clean lives. You're not going to find anything going down those roads."

"You may be right. But you're too close to the situation." Compassion softened her features, making her eyes warm. "You have to consider something in one or both of their pasts could have resulted in Chief Jameson's murder."

He hated that she was right. On both accounts. "I want that information."

With a resigned sigh, she nodded. "You can have it. I will gather everything and bring it to you tomorrow."

Taking her hand, he tugged her forward down the hall. "I need to inform Noah."

"Did you know that several criminals that

Jordan arrested have been let out of prison in the past year?"

"Of course," he threw over his shoulder.

She dug her heels into the carpet, slowing their progress. "Most left the area or are trying to make something of their lives. But there was one guy who stands out."

Carter stopped. "Who?"

"Miles Landau. He was released the day before Jordan died."

"The drug dealer. We looked at him." She really had no confidence in the department. He knew the public was restless with the lack of development in the case, he just hadn't had it brought home to him in such an in-your-face way. "His operation was shut down when he went to prison."

She raised her eyebrows. "So you know about his property on the waterfront."

Carter's gaze narrowed. "What property?"

"I uncovered a deed to a warehouse near the marina in Flushing with the business name of MiLand, Inc. Mi as in Miles and Land as in Landau. I pulled the public record on the company. MiLand, Inc. was formed two days after Miles was released from prison. And the lease on the warehouse signed a week later."

His heart rate doubled. This was new information. "You have the address?"

Lifting her chin, she nodded. "Yes, I do. And the first name of a woman, Ophelia, whom he might be seeing or staying with, though I can't seem to find her last name."

As much as he didn't want to admit it, her snooping might be helpful. And very dangerous. "Why are you doing this?"

"Doing what?"

"Looking into Jordan's murder?"

She made a face. "Reporter, remember?"

There was more to it than just her job. "But you're not being paid to write about Jordan's murder, so why? What do you hope to gain?"

"I want what everyone wants. The truth."

"You expect me to believe that's your only motive?" He shook his head. "You want to exploit my brother's death to further your career, am I right?"

"Not exploit. Never. I'm not that person." Her tone was one of pleading. "I'm doing my job. And yes, I hope if I write a great article with some meat to it, it will propel my career forward. What's wrong with that?"

"Everything, because it comes at the expense of my family."

The tenderness on her face made his stomach clench. "Your family has already paid an awful price for whatever motivated someone to kill Jordan. Don't you want the truth? It really is freeing."

Her words rang with sincerity. "What do you mean by that?"

Her expression closed, like a door slamming shut in his face. She may not realize how transparent she was, but he glimpsed the pain in her eyes before she hid it. She shrugged. "Nothing."

"Oh, something." He wasn't going to let her make a statement like that, then back away. "What truth set you free?"

"This isn't about me." She started walking down the hall. "I'd like to leave now."

He let it go. He didn't want to get invested in this woman in any way. He matched her steps. "After we tell Noah."

Noah listened, his face grim. Finally, he said, "I'll put people on Miles Landau. Though I'm skeptical he's our suspect. We looked at Miles. He doesn't have a record of violence. He's strictly low-level. However, Miss Clark, I would like to see your notes and research."

"As I told him—" she tipped her chin in Carter's direction "—I can bring it all tomorrow. It will take me some time to gather everything. I'm not the most organized individual."

Noah inclined his head. "Tomorrow, 10:00 a.m., then. I'll tell the front desk I'm expecting you. For now, I'll have Carter escort you home."

"I can't right now." Carter shook his head. "I have Ellie. Send Faith."

Noah nodded and picked up his phone to call for Officer Faith Johnson and her dog, Ricci.

"I'll leave you to it." Carter left the room without so much as a glance at Rachelle. If he never saw the reporter again, it would be too soon.

"Thank you, Officer Johnson," Rachelle stopped at the locked entrance to her apartment building.

"Of course," the petite female K-9 officer said with a smile. "I can walk you up." Her dog, a handsome German shepherd, sat patiently at her side.

Rachelle rattled the doorknob. "It's a secure building. No one can get in without a key. I'll be fine." She was exhausted. Two attempts had been made on her life. If Carter hadn't been there…

Now all she wanted was to get into her apartment before her roommates came home. A hot bath, a change of clothes and a tall glass of sweet tea were in order.

Officer Johnson looked around as if assessing the threat level. "Okay. We're just a phone call away."

Rachelle smiled because the irony was the

NYC K-9 Command Unit was so close she could probably scream and be heard by the extraordinary dogs. "I appreciate you taking time for me."

"Chief said to be back here in the a.m. to escort you to his office. I'll see you then." Officer Johnson nodded, her dark, chin-length bob moving jauntily beneath her NYPD cap.

Rachelle unlocked the door and hurried inside, making sure the door closed completely behind her and the lock was secure. Through the small square window at eye level in the door, she watched the officer and dog walk away.

Breathing out a tired sigh, she headed to the elevator only to find a handwritten note saying, Out of Order.

Great. Just what she needed. She veered away, resigned to taking the stairs to the fourth floor. She trudged up each step at a slower pace than she normally would. Her legs were tired and sore and bruised. So was her ego. All her hopes for a career boost with her investigative report into Jordan Jameson's murder had slipped out of her control.

When she told Carter about the article on his brother's murder, his expression had made her lungs constrict and even now she was struggling to catch her breath. He'd been hurt, shocked and angry. He couldn't even look at her when they were in Noah's office.

She was glad she hadn't given in to the temptation to tell him her own family drama but thankfully, she'd managed to keep it inside. He wouldn't think her issues were anything compared to the losses he'd suffered. And he was right. Her heart ached for the Jamesons.

Two flights up, she turned the corner in the stairwell and found the way blocked by a man wearing a gray T-shirt. Shock constricted the muscles in her throat. Rough hands grabbed her and spun her around so fast she didn't have time to look at his face. A muscled arm slid around her neck and squeezed while her attacker's other hand pressed a smelly cloth over her nose and mouth.

She breathed in, preparing to scream, and gagged. Her eyes watered. Her surroundings grew dim while her oxygen supply depleted, leaving her head woozy.

Her mind screamed, *Dear Lord, help me.*

FOUR

Capitalizing on the adrenaline flowing through her veins, Rachelle used what little remained of her strength to claw at the hand over her mouth and the arm squeezing her neck. She jerked her head side to side in an effort to find the crook of his elbow to relieve the pressure crushing her throat. She wildly kicked backward with the heel of her shoe and was rewarded with a grunt from her attacker.

From a floor above them a door banged open and the sound of feet on the concrete stairs echoed off the walls. Hope bubbled. *Please!*

Her attacker swore, then gruffly muttered, "Call off your investigation!"

She was abruptly thrust aside, hitting the wall with a thud while the assailant rushed down the stairwell.

Gasping for breath, Rachelle slowly slid down the wall to sit on the stairway landing and put her head between her knees.

A moment later, her upstairs neighbor, Yvette Grant, a nurse at Flushing Hospital Medical Center, appeared around the corner in her green scrubs. Rachelle had never been so happy to see anyone in—well, forever. "Yvette." The word came out a croak.

Another resounding bang reverberated off the walls as the man left the building.

"Rachelle!" Yvette knelt beside her, checking her pulse. "Are you okay?"

Rachelle shook her head. "No." She cleared her throat and pushed through the pain to add, "I need to call the police."

Yvette's dark eyes rounded. "Were you assaulted?"

"Yes." Rachelle attempted to stand.

Yvette put a restraining hand on her. "Stay where you are." She quickly dug her cell phone out of her purse and dialed 911.

"Can I talk to them?" Rachelle asked, holding out her hand.

Yvette relinquished the phone.

"Nine-one-one, what's your emergency?" a female voice answered in a calm and steady tone.

"Hello. I, uh, was attacked in my apartment building," Rachelle answered. She'd never called for help before and wasn't sure what to do or say.

"Can you give me the address?"

Rachelle recited the street number. "I'm in the stairwell."

"Are you hurt?"

Touching her tender throat, Rachelle grimaced. "Yes. Ish."

"Are you safe?"

"Yes." The question helped Rachelle collect her thoughts. She squared her shoulders. "Yes, I'm safe." *Thank You, God.* "My neighbor is here with me."

"Will the officers be able to gain access to the building?"

"No. The front door is locked." Yvette motioned she'd go downstairs. "My neighbor will let the police in."

"I'll make a note of it," the dispatcher said. "Can you tell me what happened?"

As Yvette hurried down to the lobby, Rachelle explained about the attack and that she believed it was the same man who'd pushed her off the subway platform earlier that day. "Can you inform Chief Jameson of the NYC K-9 Command Unit?"

She wondered if Carter would be told. She hoped he'd want to see that she was okay, but she knew he was angry with her and probably wouldn't care.

And that left her feeling hollow inside.

* * *

"Sweetie, go wash up and we'll have a snack," Carter told Ellie as they entered the apartment they shared with Noah on the top floor of the three-family house. Jordy's widow, Katie, had the second floor, and their parents had the ground level. Zach used to occupy one of the bedrooms in Carter's place, but after his marriage to Violet Griffin, he moved out with his bride. So now the room was a catch-all for stuff they weren't sure what to do with.

Frosty went to the water bowl in the kitchen and lapped greedily at the cool liquid. Carter didn't blame him. The heat and humidity was brutal in August.

"Okay, Daddy. Be right back." Ellie ran down the hall to the bathroom, slamming the door in her wake.

Carter winced but decided to refrain from getting after her about closing the door more gently. It was a constant battle.

Remnants of Ellie and Noah's tea party littered the small living area and kitchen space. Apparently, Noah hadn't taken time to clean up before leaving for the precinct. Resigned to taking care of it, Carter washed the tea set and placed the tiny cups, saucers and teapot on the dish drainer to dry. Cookie crumbs were scattered across the top of the miniature purple dining table in the center of the living room and on the rug. With a shake of his head, he vacuumed up the mess. When he turned off the vacuum, he heard the chime of his cell phone.

Carter glanced at the caller ID. It showed Noah's private line at the precinct.

Ellie ran into the living room. "Can I watch my show?"

Distracted, he nodded and answered the phone. "Noah?"

"Hey, just thought I'd let you know Miss Clark was attacked in her apartment building."

The news sliced through Carter. Guilt flooded the wound. "What happened? I thought Faith was escorting her home."

"She did. All seemed fine, so Faith left."

As he would have. The NYPD didn't have the resources nor the manpower to provide around-the-clock security for any one person. Almost afraid to, he asked, "Is Rachelle okay?"

"Yes. Shaken. A neighbor scared the guy off."

Relief soothed the inner chaos a bit. "Is she at the precinct?"

"No. Officers are with her at her apartment."

Pacing, Carter stated, "Whatever hornet's nest she stirred up by probing into Jordan's life brought this on." The grim knowledge made his chest tighten.

"Agreed."

"She's not safe staying in her apartment."

"Again, agreed. She needs around-the-clock protection until we can eliminate the threat to her life."

He wondered if her family could afford a private security team. "We also need her research notes. If these attacks are connected to her investigating Jordy's death…"

"Yes. Carter, I want you to handle this. Find a way to keep her safe and get the information."

Though he wasn't looking forward to seeing Rachelle again, he knew it was crucial that he press through his own issues with her being a reporter and step up to not only protect her, but also discover why she was being targeted. And he prayed in the process they would uncover the truth of his oldest brother's death.

"Text me her address, will you? Maybe Katie can stay with Ellie."

"Aren't Mom and Dad back yet?"

"I don't know. I'll check." Alexander and Ivy Jameson lived on the bottom floor of the house they'd purchased to raise their kids in. For years the two upper-floor apartments had been rentals, until the four brothers were ready to have their own space.

As the oldest, Jordan, and eventually Katie, had taken the second floor, while Carter and his late wife, Helen, had taken the top floor. But then Helen passed, leaving him to raise Ellie alone. Noah and Zach had moved up from their parents' apartment on the first floor to live with Carter and Ellie.

"Sending you Miss Clark's information now."

A short ding announced the arrival of the text. "Got it. Heading over there ASAP." He was glad he hadn't changed out of his uniform yet.

Carter clicked off the phone with his brother. "Ellie girl," he said, tucking his phone back into the pocket on his vest. "Let's go downstairs and see if Grandma and Grandpa are home."

Without hesitation, Ellie jumped off the couch and raced to the door. "Frosty," she said. "Let's go see Grandma and Grandpa."

Frosty was slower to move off his bed, but he happily trotted over to her side and squeezed past her out the door.

Carter followed the two down the staircase to his parents' apartment. Using his key to unlock the front door, he heard movement in the kitchen. Ellie raced through the rooms with a squeal of delight. Carter entered the kitchen, where his parents were unloading groceries. Frosty went in for a quick pet before settling on a large dog bed in the corner of the dining room reserved for when one of the K-9s came to visit.

Ivy Jameson smiled and held out her arms for her grandchild. "Hello, love bug!"

Ellie jumped into her grandma's arms. Carter's heart swelled. His parents had been so great. After his wife passed he had been at a loss, unsure what to do, or how he was going to raise a child on his own. His whole family had stepped up and helped. Especially his parents.

Carter greeted his mother with a kiss on the cheek and his dad with a hug.

"Would you to be willing to watch Ellie for a little bit? I've been called back in to work."

Three sets of eyes stared at him. His father nodded his understanding. The worry in his mother's eyes churned Carter's gut.

Ellie tilted her head. "Are you going to see Rachelle?"

Carter dropped his chin and stared at his little girl. How on earth had she known? "Yes, honey. I have to talk to her again."

Ellie nodded. "You need to help her some more, Daddy."

Love for his child swelled in his chest. She was so compassionate. "I will, sweetie."

"You could bring her home for dinner," Ellie said.

His mother arched an eyebrow. "Rachelle?"

Before Carter could reply, Ellie said, "She's a reporter and she fell down. Daddy's helping her. She's really pretty and I liked her—so did Frosty."

Inwardly groaning, Carter shook his head. "I'm not bringing her home."

His mom ruffled Ellie's hair. "Why don't you go into the den and set up a board game for us."

"Yippee!" Ellie ran off, leaving Carter to face his parents' questioning gazes.

"You're helping a reporter?" His dad's tone brimmed with incredulity. "They're piranhas. Why would you want to help anyone in the media?"

Knowing how frustrated his family had been by the press over the past five months, Carter understood his father's sentiment. "Dad, she's in trouble. She's mixed up in something very dangerous. She's already had three attempts on her life today."

His mother frowned. "That doesn't sound good, though it doesn't surprise me. Reporters go snooping around whether they are wanted or not."

His mother's words were so spot-on that for a moment Carter didn't have a reply.

"Can't someone else help this woman?" his dad asked.

Carter remembered the look of compassion and empathy on Rachelle's face when they'd talked about Jordan. He shook off the image. "She's in trouble and it's my job to protect her."

His mother turned away to handle the groceries. "Let somebody else be her hero. The media have raked our family over the coals enough. We don't need any more contact with reporters. And there are certainly enough police officers who could deal with her."

"I was given a direct order from Noah," Carter said. "You can take it up with him. In the meantime, yes or no to watching Ellie?"

His mother paused. "Of course we will."

His father came over to him and put his hand on his shoulder. "Use caution. Don't get caught up emotionally. Stay focused on the job."

He was emotionally involved because whatever Rachelle had stirred up had something to do with Jordan's death. But he couldn't say that to his parents.

"I'd tell you not to worry, but I know that won't stop you," he said. "So, I'll just say Frosty and I will be careful."

At the sound of his name, Frosty scrambled to his feet.

With a morose sigh he couldn't contain, Carter grasped his dad and gave him a hug. "Love you, Dad."

"We love you, son."

His mother hurried over for her own hug. "We can't lose you, too."

With a kiss to his mother's cheek, Carter stepped back. "I'll let you know when I'm headed home."

He paused at the front door to call to Ellie. "Sweetie, I'm going."

In a whirl of arms and legs, Ellie ran out of the den, where his parents had a plethora of board games and other toys for Ellie and the next soon-to-be grandchild. She launched herself into his arms. "Okay, Daddy. You be careful and take care of Rachelle."

Holding her tight, he breathed in the soft scent of her shampoo. His heart expanded in his chest. "I will." He kissed her on the top of the head and set her down. With a salute, he and Frosty exited the house.

With the dog at his heels, he jogged to the department-issued K-9 vehicle that he used to cart Frosty around. He had to park up a couple of houses because curbside parking was scarce in the neighborhood. The short driveway had room for two cars. Katie's car was already in the driveway. The other space they reserved for Noah. His parents didn't drive anymore since they preferred public transportation and walking.

He entered Rachelle's address into his GPS, hit the siren and headed out.

When he arrived at Rachelle's apartment, he was greeted by Officer Faith Johnson and her dog, Ricci.

"I feel so bad," she said. "The building was secure. There was nobody else around. I should've walked her inside. I knew it, but I had to get back to my other duties."

"You did nothing wrong. I'd have done the same thing." Though his motive for leaving wouldn't have been for the job. He'd pawned off the duty to Faith to begin with because he didn't want to have anything more to do with the reporter. Guilt wormed a hole through his conscience. "She's safe now," he continued. "That's what matters." And he would make sure she stayed that way despite his own feelings.

Faith nodded, "True. Thank you."

He and Frosty entered the building and found Rachelle sitting on the bench in the lobby talking with two plainclothes detectives. A dark-haired woman in green scrubs held her hand.

Rachelle's gaze snapped to his and the look on her face nearly upended him. *Relief? Joy?* She should be angry at him for leaving her in the lurch.

She rose and came toward him, the dirt on her gray pencil skirt and cream-colored silk blouse stark reminders of how close she'd come to being killed in the subway. The new red abrasion at her throat tied his stomach up in knots.

Stopping two feet away, she said, "I— You're here."

Frosty nudged her hand with his nose.

"Noah called me," he told her as he watched the way her fingers slid through the dog's fur in the spot behind his right ear that he loved to have scrubbed. At first glance the movement seemed casual, but she was clearly soothing herself as much as the dog. He cleared his throat before he spoke to make sure his question would come out as gently as possible. "Can you tell me what happened?"

As he listened to her story, concern grew and spread through his chest. "Are you sure it was the guy from the subway?"

She shrugged. "He had on a gray shirt. I didn't get a look at his face."

The other woman walked up, sliding her arm around Rachelle's waist. "Can she go to her apartment now?"

"And you are…?"

"This is my upstairs neighbor, Yvette Grant," Rachelle answered him. "If she hadn't come along when she had I'd be dead." A visible shiver racked her body. Frosty leaned into her, as if offering his support.

"Let me confer with the detectives." Carter

stepped aside with the two detectives and they filled each other in on the day's activities.

Detectives Sanchez and Walsh introduced themselves. Then Sanchez said, "The guy gained access to the building by posing as a floral delivery man. The forensic tech didn't find prints on the vase of carnations left in the stairwell."

"We're going to canvass the area and see if we can find where he obtained the flowers," Walsh added.

Carter handed them his card. "Keep me updated. I'll be handling Miss Clark."

The detectives nodded and left the building. Carter went to Rachelle. "Let's go get your things. You can't stay here."

"She can stay with me," Yvette offered.

Shaking his head, Carter said, "She needs to be away from this building. The assailant knows where she lives." He turned his gaze to Rachelle. She stared at him with what appeared to be shock and confusion. He explained, "We need to get you out of the city. Do you have family somewhere we can call?"

Seeming to absorb his words, she tucked in her chin. "No, I'm not calling my family."

His heart twisted in his chest. He wondered what the story was there. Obviously, they weren't close. He couldn't imagine life without his family.

"I'm not leaving New York." There was a stubborn glint in her eyes that didn't bode well. "I don't mind going to a hotel."

He sighed. "Let's discuss this in your apartment."

With a frown, she headed for the elevator.

"This was just a trick to make me take the stairs." She yanked the Out of Order sign off the door and pushed the button. A second later, the doors slid open. She stepped inside, tapped her foot and crossed her arms over her chest. "Are you coming?"

Exchanging a glance with Frosty, Carter muttered, "This is going to be fun."

FIVE

When the doors opened on the fourth floor, Carter and Frosty put a hand up to prevent Rachelle from stepping out first. He made sure the hallway was empty, then held his hand on the elevator door to keep it from closing. "We're good."

Rachelle quickly turned and hugged Yvette. "Thank you so much. You are a blessing."

"Be careful, okay?" Concern laced Yvette's voice.

"I will." Rachelle clung to her for moment, then stepped back.

Yvette shot Carter a quick glance before saying to Rachelle, "Let me know if there's anything I can do for you."

Rachelle nodded and stepped out of the elevator car. The door shut behind them. Without a word, Rachelle led Carter and Frosty to the last apartment at the end of the hall. He had to admit he admired her strength under pressure. The woman had a spine of steel.

She dug into her purse for her keys. With shaky hands, she attempted to unlock the door.

"Here, let me." As Carter took the keys, his fingers brushed over hers. She was cold, no doubt still reeling from the most recent attack. He slid the key in the lock and opened the door.

She hurried to block the way. "It's small," she warned. "We're not tidy. I have two room-mates. They share the bedroom. My domain is the living room." She bit her bottom lip, her cheeks pinkening.

Carter shrugged. "I'm not going to judge you. I live with a messy six-year-old. I just need your notes and you need to pack a bag."

Looking unconvinced, she moved aside so he could enter first. Frosty sniffed the air, then lay down, indicating there was no discernible threat.

Carter barely refrained from whistling. Okay, this was messy, beyond what three men and a six-year-old could do, back when Zach still lived with him, his daughter and Noah.

In a flurry of apparent nervousness, Rachelle grabbed the clothes on hangers dangling from the ceiling fan and hung them in the entryway closet. Then she righted the sofa bed, which had been out and unmade.

The dining room table had stacks of notebooks and loose papers, pens and highlighters, covering every square inch. Up against the wall was a freestanding whiteboard written on with notes and arrows and circles. There was a small kitchenette and a short hall with two closed doors, presumably the bath-and bedroom.

The place was hardly big enough for one person let alone three.

Moving to stand beside the dining room table, she gestured to the disorganized chaos. "Everything I have on Jordan's case is here." She gestured to the whiteboard. "And here."

He joined her by the table, taking in the looping cursive covering the pages. "You do all your notes by hand?"

"I have some things on the computer, but I think better with pen and paper. I do all my first drafts by hand, then type them in."

He couldn't imagine taking that time or having the patience to work that way. He hated doing his reports. He typed by hunt-and-peck. If he had to do them by hand, then type them in, he'd… Well, it would make for a very bad day.

"I don't know how we'll get the board out of here with just you and me," Rachelle said. "You might just want to take pictures of it."

"Good idea." He liked that she problem-solved. Taking out his cell phone, he went about the task of photographing the whiteboard.

"I'll see if I can find some boxes to throw everything into and then I can organize it later."

"That's fine. But you also need to pack your clothes."

She hesitated. "If it's not safe for me here, then it's not safe for Grace or Roxanne."

He appreciated her concern for her roommates. "You're right. They are going to need to leave, as well. Can you text or call them to let them know? They should find other accommodations for the time being."

Shoulders slumped, she nodded. "I can't believe we're having to do this."

"If you or your family can spring for a security team, then you could stay. I'm willing to wait until they arrive."

Straightening, she shook her head. "I'm not calling my family. I'll text the girls. I'm sure we can all find somewhere else to crash for a few days." She looked at him steadily. "It won't be more than a few days, will it?"

"I can't honestly say. I don't think you'll be safe coming back here to the apartment or the building. But maybe in a day or so, they can. But they can't know where you've gone."

She shuddered and dug out her cell phone from her purse. After she sent several texts, she went into the living room, where a set of dresser drawers was pushed up against the bookcase.

"Why don't you want to call your family?" For him, family was everything. He didn't know what he would do without them.

She opened some doors and stared at her clothes. "I left Georgia to be out from under their control. I'm not going to invite it back into my life."

He wasn't sure what to say. He ached for her because she obviously didn't feel supported by her family.

Turning away from the dresser, she moved to the sofa bed and knelt down on the floor to drag out a suitcase from beneath. She pulled out a couple of flat boxes, as well. He rushed over to help her.

Standing, she held out a roll of tape. "Do you mind taking care of these?"

"Not at all." He took the tape from her hand, and the boxes.

While she packed, he put together the boxes and filled them with everything on the table.

"I've taken several pictures of the whiteboard," he told her. "You need to erase it."

Leaving her suitcase by the front door, she grabbed her own phone and snapped off several images before taking a black felt eraser and wiping the board clean. "There." She set the eraser down and picked up her cell phone. "Now to find a hotel."

As Carter watched her searching the internet, Ellie's words reverberated through his head. *You better help her some more, Daddy.*

His daughter was right. He couldn't in good conscience send her off alone. And though he didn't want to do this, he knew there was only one option. "Forget the hotel. You're coming home with me."

Rachelle froze. Stunned, she lifted her gaze to meet Carter's. Surely she'd misunderstood him. He wanted to take her home? To his home? That couldn't be right. "What did you say?"

He sighed and ran a hand through his dark hair, leaving behind grooves from his strong, capable fingers. She had the craziest urge to touch his hair, to smooth down the ruffled strands. She tightened her hold on the phone.

"Listen, whatever you've stumbled on could be the break we need in solving my brother's murder. I can't leave you alone again. My family home has plenty of rooms. It's a temporary solution until we can find a secure safe house."

Her mouth dropped open. She snapped her lips together as a protest gathered on her tongue. But then her mind latched on to the fact she'd be staying with the Jamesons. Inside the family home, where she could gather more insight into Jordan's life and death.

Carter's gaze narrowed. "Don't even think about continuing with your investigation or your story."

She drew back. Had she been that transparent? "How can I stop when I've gathered more intel than the police? If you let me work with you…we could accomplish much more as a team."

He barked out a laugh. "Really? A team." Then he seemed to give it some thought. "Okay. We'll team up to go through your notes once we get back to my house."

That wasn't exactly what she meant but she'd take it for now. "Deal."

They left the apartment with Carter balancing two full cardboard boxes filled with her notes in his arms. Frosty trailed along at his side while she dragged her suitcase behind her. She appreciated that Carter had her wait to exit the elevator until after he and his partner were satisfied there were no visible threats. Her throat still burned where the man had pressed his arm against her neck and squeezed. An involuntary shudder racked her.

As if sensing the tremor racing through her, both Frosty and Carter stopped and looked at her.

"You okay?" he asked, concern darkening his blue eyes.

She swallowed past the soreness. "Yeah. Of course," she hedged, unwilling to show any weakness. She lifted a quick prayer asking for the strength to see her through this ordeal.

Carter set the boxes on the sidewalk beside his blue-and-white K-9 Unit vehicle. Using the fob on his key chain, he popped open the back hatch.

"Load up," he said.

Frosty jumped into the back compartment without hesitation.

Impressed, Rachelle said, "Wow, he really is well trained."

"We work eight to ten hours a week at the training center and then more intense specific training with others in the K-9 transit unit once a month."

"I'd really love to see the training center and witness some training. Will you be doing any drills for the upcoming K-9 trials?"

He nodded as he picked up the boxes. He gestured with his chin toward the rear passenger door. "Can you get the door?"

She opened the side back passenger door and he set the boxes on the seat, then hefted her suitcase inside, as well. He turned to look at her. "I still owe you a tour of the station house. That would include the training center. Frosty and I need to run through our obstacle courses before next Saturday."

"May I watch?" She couldn't wait to see the two in action.

He shut the back door and opened the front passenger door and leaned on the frame. "Yes. In fact, it would probably be a really good idea for you to walk the course so you can get an idea of what it's like out there."

She slid into the passenger seat, catching a whiff of his aftershave. She'd noticed the spicy, masculine scent earlier in the day. She liked the way he smelled. "That sounds fun."

"It will be." He winked and then shut the door, leaving her to wonder what he meant.

As he started the SUV, she fingered a pink scrunchie stuck in the cup holder. Ellie's, no doubt. She had to admit she was looking forward to seeing the little girl again. She was charming, just like her dad. Rachelle didn't have much experience around children. She'd never babysat like some of her friends had done during high school. Her after-school job had been office work in her father's law firm. Not that he'd paid her, saying she needed to earn her keep. She shook off the memory and paid attention to where they were going.

Carter drove them out of Forest Hills and into

Rego Park. They passed the popular four-floor shopping center with its multilevel parking garage, then wound their way through the neighborhoods of tall apartment buildings that gave way to detached homes.

He brought the vehicle to a halt in front of a three-story house with a nice front yard and beautiful full tree providing some shade.

She stared at the three-story, multifamily building. "Are the upper floors apartments?"

"Yes. Ellie, Noah and I share the top floor. Jordan and—" His voice faltered. "Katie lives on the second floor."

He climbed out before she could offer sympathy. She couldn't imagine how hard it had to be for the family to have Jordan gone and his murder unsolved.

Carter let Frosty out, then he came around to her side as she stepped out of the vehicle. He retrieved her suitcase and placed it on the paved walkway. Then he grabbed the boxes and led the way up the porch stairs to the front door.

Nerves suddenly fluttered in her stomach. "Are you sure about this?"

There was just the briefest hesitation before he said, "It'll be fine."

She wondered if he was hoping to reassure her or himself. "Did you let your family know I was coming?"

He set the boxes down and faced her. "No. My parents aren't terribly fond of reporters. The press has been less than kind to our family since Jordan's death."

She grimaced. Remembering some of the headlines. Especially in the beginning when the death at first had appeared to be a suicide. She wanted to tell him it was nothing personal. The reporters and the newspapers had a job to do. But she understood there were some who acted carelessly. She tried not to be biased one way or another in her reporting. But then again, there wasn't much to be biased about in giving an account of a new doughnut shop opening up or what a celebrity was wearing at one of the many gala events that she was assigned.

"Maybe I shouldn't be here."

"Too late. Besides, this is the best option." He opened the door and ushered her inside.

As she stepped into the house, she wondered why he was adamant that he and his family provide her shelter and security. Why not pawn her off to someone else like he'd done earlier? Guilt, she decided. He felt guilty for not having been there when she was attacked in her apartment building. "You don't have to do this."

He cocked his head. "Do what?"

"Take me in like this. It wasn't your fault I was attacked."

His mouth twisted in a rueful way that had her pulse skipping. "You caught me. I do feel guilt for not seeing you home. But bringing you here is also selfish. I want the information in these boxes."

"Ah." She wasn't sure if that made her feel better or worse. She looked away and took in the house.

The living room was cozy with well-worn leather furniture, a large-scale TV on a wood stand, shelves filled with books and magazines on the coffee table. A colorful afghan lay folded across the back of the couch. To her left was a dining room with a large dining table and enough chairs to accommodate the whole Jameson clan.

Carter set the boxes on the dining table. "You can leave your suitcase over there." He pointed to the mouth of the hallway. "Your room will be down that way. I'll show you to it after I introduce you to my parents. They're out back."

He walked through the doorway into the kitchen. With trepidation making her nerves jumpy, she followed him. Carter opened the back door and they stepped out onto a patio overlooking a grassy yard. There was a dog run and a couple of kennels. Frosty trotted straight out to the grass where two puppies, one black and one yellow with a black smudge on one ear, were chasing each other. For a moment, Rachelle watched the rambunctious pair, enraptured by the cuteness.

"Daddy!" Ellie exclaimed, scrambling out of her chair and drawing Rachelle's gaze.

An older couple and a pretty blonde also sat at the patio table, their curious gazes raking over Rachelle. Subconsciously, she smoothed her hand over her skirt wishing she'd taken the time to change into some clean clothes.

Ellie wrapped her arms around her father's waist and held him tight, and then she turned her bright blue eyes onto Rachelle. "Are you doing better now? Are you hungry?"

Disarmed, as she was earlier by the cute kid, Rachelle nodded. She was safe and famished. "Yes and yes."

Ellie released her father and slipped her hand into Rachelle's, tugging her toward the table. "Come on."

Sending Carter a questioning glance, to which he shrugged, Rachelle allowed herself to be pulled toward the table.

The elder Jameson, wearing cargo shorts and a T-shirt with the logo of the Mets emblazoned across the front, stood, his gaze locking with Carter's. He was tall, handsome and formidable. She decided the Jameson men took after their father. "Are you going to introduce your friend?"

Moving to stand beside Rachelle, Carter said, "Mom, Dad, Katie, this is Rachelle Clark." He gestured with his hand. "My sister-in-law, Katie, and my parents, Alex and Ivy."

"Hello," Rachelle said with her best smile.

She could tell from the disgruntled look on his mother's face that her presence definitely wasn't a pleasant surprise. Her blue eyes, so like her son Carter's, were wary. Her dark hair was swept up in a topknot and she wore a skort and polo top, looking comfortable and sporty at the same time. An outfit Rachelle's mother would have curled a lip at.

"Rachelle needs a safe place to stay tonight," Carter said.

"She can stay with us!" Ellie piped up.

"Actually, honey," Carter said. "I'm hoping Grandpa and Grandma can put her up in their spare bedroom."

Rachelle's gaze snapped to him. He was putting his parents on the spot. Totally uncomfortable, she said, "That's okay. I can find a hotel."

"But I want her to stay with us," Ellie protested. "She could have Uncle Zach's old room."

Carter shook his head. "No, honey, that's not going to happen." He looked to his parents. "Mom, Dad?" There was steel in his tone that made Rachelle shiver.

She didn't want to cause a rift between Carter and his family.

Carter's mother gave her a tight smile. "Of course. I'll make up the bed after dinner." She gestured toward an empty seat. "Please, join us."

Feeling as welcome as a swamp breeze, she debated turning tail and sprinting for the door. The heat of Carter's hand at the small of her back jolted through her. His gaze locked with hers. The message clear in his blue eyes said she wasn't going anywhere.

And for some reason she suddenly didn't want to leave. Which was as scary as facing down her attacker in the stairwell.

SIX

After excusing herself to take a few moments to clean up and change out of her soiled clothing into jean capris and a blue, cap sleeve shirt, Rachelle hesitated at the back door before joining the Jameson family on the patio. *What am I doing here?*

Maybe she should go home to Georgia. At least there, she knew what to expect—her parents' disapproval and assertion that she shouldn't have left in the first place. Here, she wasn't sure the Jamesons would accept her, despite the invitation to join them.

But she wasn't a quitter. And running home wasn't something she could stomach. So she squared her shoulders, lifted her chin and stepped out onto the patio.

Carter rose from his seat and held out the chair between him and Ellie. She wasn't sure what to think of that but smiled her thanks and caught Katie Jameson's curious gaze.

Rachelle's own curiosity surged. She wanted to ask Jordan's widow some questions about her husband and about their whirlwind romance, but this definitely wasn't the time or place.

"What can I get you? Hot dog or hamburger?"

Redirecting her focus, Rachelle said to Alex Jameson, "I'll take a hamburger, thank you."

Carter resumed his seat next to her, so close his knee bumped against hers. The little jolt of awareness that raced up her leg made her bounce a bit in her seat.

He looked at her, his eyebrow hitched ever so slightly, then turned to his father. "The same. With cheddar." Looking back to her he asked, "Cheese?"

Not about to tell the family she was lactose intolerant, she shook her head and simply said, "No, thank you."

For several awkward moments, there was silence so thick she could have cut it with a butter knife. Then Ellie started chattering about ponies. And the two puppies raced around beneath their feet, making everyone laugh. Rachelle began to relax, enjoying the novelty of a loud and boisterous family dinner. Her hamburger was tasty and satisfying. Much better than the salad she'd planned on having tonight.

"Miss Clark, where do you come from?" Ivy

asked. "There's just a little bit of an accent in your voice."

Ugh. The stress of the day had her slipping and rendering her diction practice useless. She tried to modulate her voice as she answered, "I'm from Georgia."

"Ah. We haven't ventured much to the southern states. New York must be a whole different way of life to you," Ivy commented.

She inadvertently caught Carter's gaze. She didn't know how but she was certain he was thinking of her sprawled flat on the sharp gravel between the tracks of a subway train, waiting in terror for what might be a horrible death. She blinked away the awful image and gave him, then his mother, a toothy smile. "Yes, but I'm getting used to it. I like the fast-paced lifestyle. Much different from the small town where I grew up."

"Your family must miss you," Ivy said.

Rachelle figured they hardly noticed her absence. They barely paid attention when she was around except to find fault with her. For the way she dressed, the way she wore her hair or talked. She never was able to live up to their expectations.

"She doesn't have contact with her family," Carter interjected.

Slanting him a glance, Rachelle inhaled sharply. She didn't appreciate him answering for her.

Carter lifted an eyebrow.

"We aren't speaking at the moment," she said. She didn't tell him that she'd uncovered a secret that had not only explained many things for her but also caused a rip through the fabric of their family.

Thankfully, the subject matter changed to the Jamesons' recent visit to Fire Island and the upcoming K-9 trials. Rachelle soaked it all in, deciding she would have to take a trip to see the lighthouse at the tip of Long Island. And the more she heard about the K-9 trials the more excited she was to write about the event.

Ellie tapped her on the shoulder and leaned over. In a loud whisper, she said, "Will you come to the K-9 trials and sit with me? It's so much fun to watch Daddy and Frosty. They do some funny things."

"That's my plan, Ellie." Touched by the child's requests, she added, "I'd love to sit with you. If it's okay with your dad."

Ellie grinned. "It's okay, right, Daddy?"

"Yes, sweetie," Carter answered, his gaze meeting Rachelle's.

She couldn't decipher what had him looking so intense.

"Daddy, may I be excused now?" Ellie asked.

"I ate well." There were just a few little remnants of her hot dog and potato salad on her plate.

"You did good," Carter agreed. "You may be excused."

Ellie raced down the porch stairs to play in the grass with the two little Labrador puppies, while Frosty watched from beneath the shade of an awning.

Katie stood, picking up her plate and her father-in-law's, then started into the house.

Needing something to do, Rachelle followed suit, gathering the empty plates. "I'll help you."

She hesitated before taking Ivy's plate.

The older woman gave her an assessing glance before lifting the plate to stack it on top of the others in Rachelle's hands. "That's very sweet of you, dear."

"The least I can do," Rachelle replied with a smile. "I need to earn my keep."

Ivy smiled back, her features softening. "That is not necessary."

Unsure how to respond, Rachelle followed Katie into the kitchen, where Katie set the plates in the sink. For a moment, she leaned against the counter rubbing her back.

Stacking her own pile of dishes in the sink, Rachelle eyed Katie with concern. "Are you okay?"

"Yes. I just battle with bouts of fatigue. It's been a very emotional five months."

Empathy spread through Rachelle's chest. "I can imagine. I'm so sorry that you're going through this."

Katie turned on the water faucet and rinsed the dishes before putting them into the dishwasher. "Not much I can do but pray Jordan's killer is caught."

"Here, let me do that." Rachelle shooed Katie aside. She took over rinsing the plates and silverware and putting them into the dishwasher. "I'm sure something will break in the case soon." She glanced out the window over the sink, making sure that Carter was still with his parents. She turned off the faucet and turned to Katie. "I'm actually working on a story about your husband's death. That's why I'm here."

Katie frowned. "What do you mean?"

"Carter will probably get mad at me for telling you this, but the attempt on my life today must have something to do with my investigation into Chief Jameson's murder."

Katie put a hand on the counter as if the news had weakened her knees. "I don't know what to say."

Noticing that Katie's face had lost its color, Rachelle dragged a chair in from the dining room. "You should sit."

Katie sank onto the wooden chair. "I feel like I've let Jordan down. I promised myself

I wouldn't rest until they found out who killed him. But to be honest, these days, resting is about all I can do. I'm glad you're investigating. But I don't like the fact that your life is in danger."

Rachelle felt better about her investigation knowing that Katie appreciated her efforts. "Thank you for saying that. Carter's not terribly happy with me, but at least he's willing to team up."

Katie tilted her head, a speculative gleam in her eyes. "Team up, huh? That's interesting. He must really like you."

"I don't think 'like' is the right word. He finds me an irritant. He's only working with me for my notes. If he could read them without my help, I wouldn't be here."

"What do you mean?"

"A lot of my notes are written in my own form of shorthand. I'm the only one who can transcribe them."

Katie nodded approvingly. "Clever girl. And I'm not sure you're correct in thinking Carter finds you irritating," she said with a smile. "He went all he-man with his parents over you. I've never seen him do that before."

Hoping to change the subject, Rachelle asked, "Do you know if you're having a boy or girl?"

Katie put her hand on her tummy. "A girl."

Tears gathered in Katie's eyes. "Jordan so wanted to be a father."

Aching for her, Rachelle said, "It's really good that you have so much support from the Jameson family."

Katie nodded and wiped her eyes. "Yes, they've been really great. My own parents are long gone. Everybody has been so kind to me. A couple of ex-boyfriends and several coworkers have all offered to help in some way or another. Even my college roommate, who I'd lost touch with when she moved to Europe, made contact and said I could go live with her if I needed."

"Would you go?"

Katie shook her head. "No. This is my family now." She rubbed her belly. "Our family."

"You're a teacher, correct?" Rachelle vaguely remembered something about Katie's job in one of the articles she'd read after Jordan's death.

"Yes, fifth grade at Rego Park Elementary School. Though I'd resigned for this coming school year as Jordan wanted me to be a stay-at-home mom." She sighed. "Maybe I'll go back to teaching once the baby is old enough. Ivy has offered to provide day care."

"I'm sure Mrs. Jameson is looking forward to taking care of another grandchild."

"Oh yes. I don't know what I would do without Alex and Ivy. Of course, Carter and Ellie and Noah will be here to help out. Zach and his new wife, Violet, have offered to pitch in, as well. Like I said, family."

"I have to confess I envy your close-knit family."

"I married into it," Katie said. "My parents died years ago." She tilted her head. "Why are you not on speaking terms with your family?"

The ache and hurt from learning she was adopted reared up to clog her throat. She wasn't ready to talk about learning the reason she was never accepted by the man and woman she'd called her mother and father. "It's complicated."

"Do you have siblings?" Katie asked.

"I'm an only child. I was a surprise that came along later in my parents' life." An unwanted guest that stayed too long. "They had chosen not to have children. But apparently, God had other plans."

"There's no arguing with God and His plans," Katie said. "I'm sure He has great things in store for you."

Liking Katie and appreciating her kind words, Rachelle smiled. "Thank you for that."

"So, are you married? Dating anyone?"

"No, to both questions. I'm focusing on my career right now."

"There's no reason you can't be married and have a career," Katie pointed out.

"Maybe someday," Rachelle said. "But not anytime soon."

"What do you think of Carter?"

Oh no. She was trying to play matchmaker. Not happening. "Please don't go there." Remembering the wedding photo on his desk, she added, "I get the sense that he's still mourning his late wife."

"Perhaps. I never met Helen. But from what everybody has told me of her she was a wonderful person. It would take a special person to replace her." Katie tilted her head, her gaze speculative. "I have a feeling you could be that person."

The back door opened, and Carter stepped inside. His gaze bounced between Rachelle and Katie and back again. "What's going on?"

Cheeks flaming, Rachelle quickly went back to the dishes. "Nothing."

Rachelle reminded herself not to get attached to him or his beautiful little daughter. Because there was no way she could be special enough to fill the empty hole left by his wonderful wife.

The next day Carter packed the boxes back into his SUV and he and Rachelle and Frosty headed to the NYC K-9 Command Unit headquarters.

Rachelle had been quiet the rest of last evening and again this morning as they prepared to leave. He'd asked her to wear comfortable clothing for their trip to the training center. He tried not to notice how cute she looked in her loose-fitting pants and T-shirt with the words Hello Sunshine written across the front.

She had been a ray of sunshine last night. The way Ellie and Katie responded to her made his heart glad that he'd brought her home, despite his mother's less than warm welcome. Mom could be a tough cookie, but he knew she'd warm up to Rachelle in time. Not that he needed her to for his sake. Far from it.

When he'd walked into the kitchen to find Rachelle and Katie talking, it was the first time in a long time that Katie hadn't looked to be on the verge of tears.

Of course Ellie adored Rachelle. Too much, in fact. All Ellie could talk about as he was putting her to bed was Rachelle. *Isn't she pretty, Daddy? Isn't she so nice, Daddy?*

And when Ellie asked if Rachelle would come and sit with her at the K-9 trials, he had to fight the need to warn both of them not to get attached. He just hoped he could end the threat to Rachelle sooner rather than later so they could all go back to their normal, separate lives.

He pulled into the parking lot behind the brick building housing the NYC K-9 Command Unit.

After releasing Frosty from the vehicle and attaching his lead, Carter hefted the two cardboard boxes into his arms.

She reached for the top one. "I can carry that. You don't have to do it all yourself."

For the briefest moment he thought of protesting. But then decided she was right. And it would free him up just a bit in case he needed to drop the box if something were to happen between here and the precinct. He nodded. "Thanks. I appreciate it."

Her smile reached her eyes this time. He liked the way her brown eyes lit up and crinkled at the corners when she was genuinely smiling.

Frosty nudged his leg, drawing his attention. The dog no doubt wanted to know why they weren't on the move. Because he was enjoying staring into Rachelle's eyes. He mentally gave himself a shake and started walking.

Carter stopped at the training center to drop Frosty off with the lead trainer.

He could tell Rachelle wanted to linger. "We'll come back here later."

She nodded and followed him to Noah's office. He'd come home late last night and left again before Carter had gotten up to get Ellie ready for an outing with his parents.

"I take it those are your case notes," Noah

said, eyeing the boxes they held as they entered the room.

"Yes, sir. As promised," Rachelle responded.

Carter liked that she wasn't a shrinking flower. She was bold and strong. She had to be if she was digging into his brother's death. Acid churned in his gut. Something in one of these boxes would lead them to the truth.

"Take the conference room," Noah instructed. "Shut the blinds. I don't want anybody interfering." He leveled Carter with a direct look. "This is for your eyes only. Not even Dad or Zach."

Surprise washed through Carter. His brother's confidence in him was pleasing. He gave Noah a sharp nod and led the way to the conference room. For the next several hours, he and Rachelle went about the task of laying all the notes out. Some of her writing was indecipherable to him.

"My shorthand," she said. "I learned from my father's law clerk."

"Your father's a lawyer." Lawyers were right up there with reporters as far as he was concerned. Good when you needed them, but the rest of the time he wanted nothing to do with them.

"Can you un-shorthand them so I can read them?"

"Of course I can. It will take some time. Might be easier if I just read the notes to you."

"Good idea. Let's try that." He grabbed his pad to take notes of his own.

She took a seat and picked up a ledger. "Recent releases from the jail system." She read the list of names in her slightly accented voice that filled the room. She had a nice voice and he had to concentrate to stay focused on listening to the words and not just the warm, honeyed tone.

Partway down the list was Miles Landau. But there were other names he hadn't heard before. He lifted a hand. "Hold up. All of those inmates had some connection to Jordan?"

"Yes. Going back through public records." She put emphasis on the word *public*. "Jordan was involved in each of these cases in some way. In some he was the first responder to the scene. Those are from back when he was a rookie. Other cases as the arresting officer, while in many he was the officer in charge of the investigation."

Carter tumbled that information through his head. Could Jordan's death have something to do with a case from the past?

"Okay." He decided to pursue this line of thought. "You've pulled case files on each of these ex-cons?"

"I have. Many of their files are very thick and some not so much. Several were a slam dunk, while others the state had to really dig deep to convict. I've also dug into various social media outlets to see what I could find about where they are now and what they are doing."

She was a go-getter; he'd give her that. "Let's start at the top and dig our way through all of the files."

"You don't want to start with Miles? He was released the day before your brother's death. And I have the most information on him. Photos from before he was incarcerated and after."

"We have no way of knowing if he's the culprit. It could be any one of these guys."

"My instincts tell me Miles is up to something," she insisted. She handed him a photo of the man standing on the deck of what looked like a fancy boat, a bottle of alcohol in one hand and a pretty woman next to him.

Carter wasn't sure he trusted her instincts. He stared at the photo. Was this man responsible for Jordan's death? "Noah put a man on finding and trailing Landau. If he makes any strange moves, we'll know."

For a moment, he thought she'd continue to argue but instead she took the picture back and replaced it in the file.

"All right, then." She read the top name again. "This guy was a pusher who beat his girlfriend. The state's case against him put him away on drug charges as well as attempted murder. Your brother was the first officer on the scene."

"Tell me everything you could find out about him."

The ring of a cell phone echoed off the conference room walls.

"That's me," Rachelle said. "Sorry. I thought I turned the ringer off." She hurried to where she'd hung her purse across the back of a chair and answered the phone. "Hello."

At that exact moment, Noah opened the conference room door, his expression grim. "We have a situation."

Carter went to his brother, while keeping his eyes on Rachelle. Her face had gone white at whatever was said on the other side of the cell phone conversation. He heard her exclaim, "Oh no! I'll be right there."

Carter's gaze whipped to his brother as dread cramped his chest. "What's going on?"

The hard set of Noah's mouth sent unease sliding through Carter.

"There was a break-in at the *NYC Weekly* offices." Noah tipped his chin toward Rachelle. "Her desk space specifically was targeted."

Carter's gut clenched. "Whoever was after her wanted these notes."

"My thought exactly," Noah said.

Rachelle rushed to the door with her purse slung over her shoulder. "I have to go. It's the office."

"I know," Carter said. "Come with me to get Frosty and we'll head over there."

"I can't wait!" She slipped past him and Noah and hurried toward the front staircase.

"Go get your partner," Noah instructed him. "I'll keep her from leaving without you."

Carter peeled away and headed down the back stairwell to the training center while Noah went after Rachelle.

Frosty was sleeping in a kennel but as soon as Carter stepped into the large space reserved for the dogs to have some downtime, Frosty rose and stretched. Carter let him out of the kennel. "Time to work, boy."

Without a word, the lead trainer, Olivia King, handed him a lead.

"Thanks." He leashed up and hustled out of the kennel room.

"Be safe," Olivia called after him.

"From your lips to God's ears," he muttered beneath his breath.

When Carter and Frosty reached the lobby, Noah was talking to Rachelle, hopefully keeping her from acting impulsively. She tapped her foot as he approached.

Noah waved him on. "Go."

With a nod, Carter led Rachelle and Frosty

through the exit. Because her office building was only a few blocks away, they didn't need to drive. The sidewalk was crowded as they joined the flow of pedestrians. They reached the intersection just as the Walk sign flashed.

Up ahead, the sidewalk was blocked by a hand truck stacked with aluminum kegs. He slowed, hoping to give the workers time to get the hand truck out of the way.

"We have to go around them," Rachelle insisted and stepped off the curb, skirting past the parked cars.

Clenching his jaw, he and Frosty followed but were waylaid by pedestrians taking the same route in the opposite direction.

At the next corner, a white panel van pulled up in front of Rachelle, blocking her path. The side door opened and two men with ski masks covering their faces jumped out. She skidded to a halt and attempted to backpedal, but the men grabbed her by the arms to drag her into the van.

SEVEN

Carter's heart jumped into his throat at the sight of the two men grabbing Rachelle. He surged forward, through the crowd. "Police. Move!" He dropped Frosty's leash as he ran. "Attack!"

Carter trusted the dog's training to know the difference between the aggressor and the victim in this situation. Plus, Frosty knew and loved Rachelle.

Frosty raced to launch himself at the closest kidnapper. The dog's powerful jaw snapped closed and his teeth sank into the man's forearm through his black long-sleeved windbreaker. The guy screamed with pain behind his black ski mask, releasing his hold on Rachelle as he tried to shake off Frosty.

With her free hand, she landed a well-placed punch to the second man's face. Blood spurted through the nose hole of his mask after she made contact. He dropped her arm to grab his face. She pivoted and ran toward Carter.

The two men, one still struggling with Frosty, jumped back into the panel van as the driver hit the gas. Frosty ran alongside, still clamped onto the man's arm as he screamed, punching and kicking in a useless effort to force Frosty to let go.

Fearing for his partner's safety as the van picked up speed, practically dragging Frosty, Carter yelled, "Out!"

Immediately, Frosty released his hold on the man and veered in an arc back to Carter's side as the van's panel door closed and the vehicle sped away. Carter had no way to follow, but he noted the plates were missing, like the sedan. These guys were making it hard.

Wrapping his arms around Rachelle, Carter took deep breaths, willing his heart to slow down. Within his embrace, her body shook. Frosty leaned against Rachelle's legs as if offering his support.

"You're safe. I've got you." He couldn't believe his voice sounded so calm, because inside he was quaking. Witnessing another assault on Rachelle nearly stripped him to the very core. He couldn't let anything happen to this woman.

Ellie would never forgive him.

He would never forgive himself.

She lifted her frightened gaze to his and

curled her fingers around his flak vest. "How did they know I'd be here?"

"I can only guess the break-in was also a way to flush you out," he told her.

Keeping an arm wrapped securely around her, he radioed in the incident, telling Dispatch to put the van's description out to all units and to call the area hospitals alerting them to watch for a man with a dog bite on his left arm and another man with a broken nose.

Picking up the leash with his free hand, Carter hustled them toward her office building. Caution tape barred the entrance. He nodded at the officer standing guard, who lifted the tape for them, allowing them access. Once inside the building, Rachelle led him to her cubicle. The drawers of her desk were upended, and her computer hard drive gone.

Carter's stomach sank. He leaned in close to her ear. "Please tell me you didn't back up all your work onto your office computer."

She shook her head. "No. I told you, I've been working on this at home. Never here."

For that he was grateful.

"Rachelle," a deep voice called.

She pushed past Carter and Frosty and hurried to where a man with salt-and-pepper hair stood in an open doorway. The placard next to the door read Editor in Chief.

"Are you okay?" the man said. "I just heard two men tried to kidnap you."

"I'm fine, Quinn, thank you. Is everyone here okay?"

"Yes. The break-in happened overnight."

"I don't know what to say. I'm so, so sorry this happened."

"This isn't your fault," he said.

"Yes, actually it is," she replied. "I've been working on a side project looking into Chief Jordan Jameson's murder."

Carter was proud of her for taking ownership.

Quinn's bushy eyebrows rose. "You don't say." He shook his head. "I told you to let it go. But since you didn't, you can fill me in on what you have."

Carter stepped forward. "Sir, this is a police matter. And confidential. I will be taking Miss Clark with me."

The man sized Carter up. "Is she in trouble?"

Before Carter could respond, Rachelle said, "This is Officer Carter Jameson. Jordan Jameson's brother."

Carter wouldn't have thought it possible but the older man's eyebrows rose even higher, nearly disappearing into his hairline.

"Indeed."

Rachelle turned to Carter. "This is my boss, Quinn Seidel."

Carter stuck out his hand. "Mr. Seidel."

"Officer. My condolences on your brother."

Extracting his hand, Carter turned to Rachelle. "We need to get going."

She nodded but turned back to her boss. "I'm still going to cover the K-9 trials and the celebrity ball. Please, don't take these assignments away from me."

Carter stared at her. Really? That's what she was worried about? Her assignments? Figured. Her ambition went before anything else. He would be wise to remember that.

"I don't know," Quinn said. "I—"

"Carter is helping me with the K-9 article," Rachelle quickly interjected. She gave Carter a pleading look. "Right?"

Jaw tightening, Carter nodded. He still needed her help to decipher her notes. "Yes."

She swung back to Quinn. "See? And he's going to escort me to the ball."

Carter choked on a laugh. "What?"

Her brown gaze implored him to agree. "As my bodyguard." She mouthed the word *please*.

His mouth dried. Every instinct inside of him screamed for him to decline her request but he thought of Ellie and how disappointed she would be if he refused to help Rachelle.

"Is that correct, Officer Jameson? You'll be in attendance at the ball?" Quinn asked. His piercing blue eyes assessed Carter. "It would be good to have a police presence there considering all the mayhem going on these days."

Rachelle gave him an impish smile that did funny things to his insides.

"Yes. Fine. I'll be escorting Rachelle to the ball."

Putting her hands in a prayer position, Rachelle mouthed, *thank you*. She turned back to her boss. "I'd like to work remotely for a while if that's okay."

Quinn narrowed his gaze for a moment, then relented. "That's probably for the best."

Carter wasn't sure whom it would be best for.

With another officer in tow, Carter ushered Rachelle and Frosty into the veterinarian clinic, where the vet, Dr. Ynez Dubios, gave him a thorough once-over and determined he'd suffered no injuries while protecting Rachelle.

Grateful for his partner's clean bill of health, Carter felt the tightness in his chest ease as they walked the short distance to the station. When they reached the lobby, he paused. "You should talk to the psychologist the department uses," he said to Rachelle. "Dr. Benchley is really good at helping victims process their feelings."

"You're very thoughtful to think of it," she said, her gaze tender. "I wouldn't mind talking to someone."

Glad he'd had the idea, he ushered her to the desk sergeant and got the phone number for Dr. Brenda Benchley.

She tucked the number in her purse. "I'll give her a call later to set up an appointment."

His stomach rumbled with hunger, reminding him they'd missed lunch. "Let's grab food from the commissary and then head to the training center, where Frosty can get some water. We can eat down there, too, and you can make the call."

She gave him a wan smile. "I'm not sure I can eat right now."

"You need to at least try," he told her. "Keep up your strength."

Securing the strap of her purse higher over her shoulder, she said, "I could go for another of your father's hamburgers. He does barbecue right."

Carter laughed, glad for the lighter topic. "He's a master at it."

"Has he taught you how to grill?"

"All of us had to learn. Not only how to barbecue but to mow the lawn and fix what needed repair. 'No slackers in my house,' Dad would say."

"I'll bet he made it fun, though," she said with a wistful tone. "You all bonded over projects."

He gave her a sideways glance as they took the stairs down to the basement level. Frosty's nails clicked on the cement steps. "Yes, we did bond. He was really good about making sure we each got one-on-one time with him throughout the years."

"That's really special."

Love for his father infused his voice. "Yes. He's been a good dad. A good role model both personally and professionally. He and my grandfather were both NYPD."

"The family business."

"There were also times when Dad made the four of us kids cooperate and work together." Remembering those times brought an ache to his chest. Now there were only the three of them left. "*Teamwork*, was another of his big phrases. Of course, Mom used teamwork to mean housework."

"You were blessed to have such involved parents."

In the commissary, they grabbed salads and bottles of water and took their bounty to the training center, where he dropped Frosty off with Olivia for some water.

"We'll be back shortly," Carter told Frosty.

"Do you always talk to him like a human?" Rachelle asked as she followed Carter to the break room.

He shrugged as he settled into a chair. "Dogs understand way more than we can know. I read a study once that claimed dogs processed words with the left side of their brains just like humans and they use the right side of their brains to understand tone and pitch."

"That's fascinating," she said, taking a seat next to him. "I had no idea. I never had a pet growing up."

Carter couldn't imagine not having an animal to care for. Dogs had been such an integral part of his life.

"Tell me about your family," he said as he unwrapped his salad. He hoped to keep her talking while the rush of adrenaline from earlier ebbed away. "Why are you not speaking?"

She made a face. "It's a long story."

"We have time."

"Dad was a prominent lawyer in town until he retired last year. Mom…" She hesitated, pushing her lettuce around with her fork. "She likes to be involved." There was an edge to her voice. "She volunteers for any committee she can. She likes to keep busy."

"Your dad retired young," he commented.

"They were older when I—" She seemed lost in thought.

"Was born?" he prompted.

She let out a humorous laugh. "Yes. My parents are actually my aunt and uncle."

"Okay."

She set down her fork. "I didn't know I was adopted until college. I was doing a paper on my family genealogy and discovered my birth was a scandal. Lily Clark, my father's youngest sister, was unmarried when she had me."

He covered her hand with his. "You must have been shocked and hurt."

"Yes." Her lips twisted. "Once I knew, so many things made sense. Like why I could never measure up to my mother's standards."

"What happened to your birth mother?"

A sad light entered her gaze. "She perished in a car accident while I was still an infant. My dad took me in, but my mother hadn't wanted children."

He squeezed her hand. "I'm sorry."

She smiled. "It is what it is."

He realized her smile was her default mode when she wanted to keep an emotional distance. His heart ached for her.

"I had a string of nannies, none of which stayed long, because, well, I didn't make life easy for them."

"You liked to climb giant trees and fall out," he said, remembering her story about the oak tree.

"Little girls were not supposed to do things like that. But I did everything I was not supposed to do. Nothing criminal, but certainly nothing deemed proper by my parents. Even my choice of college went against their wishes. I attended the state school instead of a prestigious private one."

"I'm surprised they didn't push you to get married and have children," he said, not liking the picture she was painting of her parents.

She glanced at him sharply. "Oh, they tried. They even picked out someone for me. Wallace Thompson." She set her fork down, leaving her salad untouched. "I dated him, trying to be the good daughter, hoping for Mom's and Dad's approval." She blew out a breath. "But I realized Wallace just wanted a partnership in my dad's law firm. He didn't really care about me, and I certainly didn't love him. So I broke it off and moved to New York. I decided to focus solely on my career."

"Good for you. Though I find your choice of career lamentable."

She cocked an eyebrow. "As do I yours."

He drew back. "What?"

Her gaze was direct. "You have a daughter. Why would you stay in a career that puts you in harm's way? Look what happened to your brother. Now Katie's left to raise their child alone. What if something happened to you? Ellie would lose her father, too."

Her words sliced through him like a double-edged sword. "That's not fair. Life and death happen. We can't control any of it."

He'd learned the harsh lesson the hard way as he'd watched his wife die in childbirth. And now Jordan was gone, too.

Sorrow burned at the back of his eyes.

He battled back the anger at God for allowing Helen to die that occasionally tried to surface. The grief counselor Carter had seen in the first few years after her death had helped him to see that blaming God instead of turning to Him for comfort only heightened the pain. Believing that God grieved with him was the only way he made it through the dark days.

Rachelle reached across the table and covered his hand. "You've lost so much. I'm so sorry."

He stared at their joined hands. Her hand so much smaller and feminine compared to his large, rough paw. Warmth spread up his arm from the contact. He couldn't remember the last time he'd let anyone close who wasn't family. He couldn't let himself become involved with this woman.

She flexed her fingers; the pressure against his wrist made his pulse jump.

"We're going to find the answers. We'll solve your brother's murder. Together. Like a team."

He swallowed as he fell into her brown-eyed gaze. For five months with no leads, he'd almost given up that they would bring Jordan's killer to justice. He hated that there were crimes that people got away with, that were never solved. He'd prayed that Jordan's death would not be one of them. And this woman's assurance that, together, they could do what a whole department couldn't, bolstered his flagging hopes and made him want to believe in her, in them, as a team.

But he couldn't let himself become emotionally attached to this woman. Or any woman. He had no intention of opening himself up again to the kind of loss he'd experienced when Helen died.

He cleared his throat and pulled his hand out from beneath hers. "Temporarily a team. Only until we have answers and find the person who wants you dead."

The sparkle left her eyes. "Right. Of course."

Carter noticed Rachelle had barely taken more than a few bites of her salad as they cleaned up the remnants of their lunch. He figured his reminder of the danger she was in had stolen her appetite. He dismissed the idea that she was upset that he'd made it clear they were only a temporary team. She had to know this was a onetime thing. And for the sole purpose of keeping her safe and finding his brother's killer.

They returned to the conference room but neither of them could concentrate. Rachelle kept reading the same words over and over and it wasn't until the fourth time he heard the repeated sentence that he realized they weren't progressing. Finally, he held up his hand. "Rachelle, take a break."

"I'm sorry," she said, looking dejected. "I'm struggling."

She needed a distraction. They both did, because he was having the same problem. He kept reliving the moment the van pulled up and the two men grabbed her. If not for Frosty...

He rose and held out his hand. "Come with me."

There was a brief hesitation before she slipped her hand into his. It felt natural and right to have their hands clasped together. He was reluctant to let go when he locked up the conference room and pocketed the key. Tucking his thumbs into his utility belt to keep from reaching for her again, he escorted Rachelle to the kennel room, where they picked up Frosty. As soon as the kennel door opened, the dog went to Rachelle, his tail wagging as he leaned against her legs.

"He seems to really like you," Carter said, a bit flummoxed by the dog's show of affection.

She rubbed Frosty in the perfect spot behind his ears. His eyes practically rolled in his head with bliss.

Shaking his head, Carter said, "This way. I want to show you something."

He led the way to the center of the training floor covered in Astroturf. There were several obstacles set up. Not as many as they'd run through during the upcoming K-9 trial but enough to keep them sharp.

"I've watched a little agility on TV," Rachelle said as she took in the training equipment. "These don't look like normal agility obstacles."

"They're not." He gestured toward the eight-foot-long wooden tunnel. "The crawl obstacle is for when we have tight spaces only the dogs can get through, like under a porch or in a culvert." He pointed to three large crates with windows cut out at the top on all four sides. "Those three boxes in the middle of the room are for scent work. Meaning, during competition, somebody will hide in a crate and then Frosty will have to find which crate the person is in."

She dug out her pink flower notebook from her purse. And started scribbling in it as he talked. Frosty lay down at her feet.

Eyeing his partner, Carter continued, "This helps us when we're doing searches and we have a suspect who thinks he's going to hide in a garbage can or in the vents of a building. Humans give off more than just body odor. Their scent is released every time they breathe and every time their skin cells drop off their body."

"This is great stuff," she said. "I can't wait to write this article. Oh, pictures. Would you mind if I take some?"

"You'd be better off waiting until the actual trials. Those will be much more interesting and dramatic. These are only a fraction of what we'll be doing in competition."

"Right. Good point." She gestured to the other side of the floor's center. "What about that wall with the window? Does someone hide on the other side of that?"

"No. Frosty has to go through the window."

She stared at Frosty. "He can jump that high?"

"I give him a boost. Part of being a K-9 handler is making sure that we can lift our dogs while at the same time having the fifty or so pounds of equipment strapped to our body."

She whistled. "That's crazy." She wrote it down.

"It's necessary. We're going to run the course so you can see how it works. And then you are."

She barked out a laugh. "You're not serious."

He rubbed his hands together. "Yes, I am."

"There's no way I can lift that dog high enough to go through the window."

"Don't worry. I'll make sure you can do it."

She gave him a doubtful look. "I'm glad you're so confident."

"I am. You might want to stand over by the door. Once we get going you don't want to be in the way."

She nodded and hustled to plaster her back against the wall. Her pen poised over her notebook.

He patted his side and Frosty lined up next to him. In tandem, they walked to the far end of the training center.

"Sit." Frosty obeyed. Carter stepped away then said, "Find."

Frosty ran around the room, with his nose bouncing from the floor to the air. He went to the boxes and sat down in front of the far right one. Carter went over and opened a latch that allowed a door to open. Inside he found a small blue bucket filled with liver treats that Olivia kept inside. "Good boy." He gave the dog a treat.

"What did he find?" Rachelle called out.

He held up the bucket. "The dog knows where his snacks are."

She smiled and wrote in her notebook. He put the treats back.

As he patted his side, Frosty fell into step with him. They lined up for the crawl and the jump to the window. "Go!" They both ran as fast as they could, and then Frosty squeezed through the open end of the crawl space. Carter met his partner at the other end. They ran for the window.

Frosty jumped into the air, his front paws reaching for the windowsill. Carter caught him by the haunches and lifted Frosty the rest of the way. The dog leaped through the opening, landing easily and circling back to Carter's side.

Rachelle clapped. "That was amazing."

"Now your turn."

She shook her head. "Not a chance."

"You can do it. Put your purse down and come here." He cocked an eyebrow. "Or are you too chicken?"

Her mouth popped open in obvious indignation. She snapped her lips together and laid her purse on the floor. "All right, hotshot. Show me how this works."

Gratified to see her taking his challenge, he said, "Call Frosty to your side by patting your outer thigh. And call his name."

She did as instructed. Frosty's gaze bounced between Rachelle and Carter. He nodded, giving the dog permission, and Frosty trotted over to her side and sat beside her.

Her face lit up with delight and Carter's breath stalled in his chest. Shaking his head, he stepped to the side. "When you're ready, say *go*. Then you're going to run as fast as you can to the crawl. While he's taking the tunnel, you keep running toward the window. He'll meet you there."

Her eyebrows dipped together. "And you expect me to lift him?"

"You help push him up and through. I'll be right alongside you."

She grinned. "Just like a team."

"Like a team."

She took a deep breath and said, "Go." She ran. Frosty darted forward with Rachelle racing behind. Carter couldn't keep from grinning as he ran alongside her. Frosty took the crawl. When he emerged, Carter gave him a hand signal to slow down since Rachelle hadn't reached the window yet.

Once she was there, Carter motioned for Frosty to take the window. As he leaped, Rachelle reached out to place her hands on his haunches. Carter moved in to help, his hands covering hers. Together, they boosted Frosty through the opening.

Rachelle clapped her hands, a big smile on her face. "That was fun. And you do that with all your gear on? I am so impressed."

Pleased by her praise, he said, "I'm glad you enjoyed it. Your story will sound authentic now."

"You're right. I appreciate you doing this for me." The warmth in her gaze sent his heart pounding. The air around them seemed electrified. Frosty nudged him in the back of the knee. He took a step toward her as alarm bells went off in his head.

"Uh, we should get back to work." He spun away and strode toward the door, his heart pounding in his chest like he was sixteen again.

EIGHT

"I'm telling you we should be looking closer at Miles Landau and finding this Ophelia woman. She might know something," Rachelle stated, referring to the name that she'd uncovered in a social media post by Miles before his incarceration six years ago. Why wouldn't Carter listen to her?

They sat across from each other at the conference table. He'd brought Frosty with them and the dog lay across her feet, keeping her toes warm in the air-conditioned room. Her eyes felt gritty from looking through her notes and her throat was sore from reading most of her handwritten pages aloud to Carter.

"Noah has Miles under surveillance." His voice held a sharpness to it.

Ever since they had returned to the conference room after running the obstacles with

Frosty, Carter had been distant with clipped answers and hardly looking at her.

Which seemed so odd considering she'd thought they were connecting in the training center. He'd been so kind to provide her a distraction from the horror of nearly being abducted.

But what did she know? He was a confusing man. All protective and caring then standoffish and brooding. She decided the stress of the case and the attempts on her life were making them both tense and edgy.

He sighed, long and loud, as if he'd just lost an argument he'd been having with himself, then he spoke as if he was explaining something to a very slow-witted person. "I ran the name Ophelia through the national database," he continued. "Nothing noteworthy popped. Danielle, our computer tech, has been cross-referencing the name with Miles but hasn't come up with anything. The name probably refers to the new rooftop bar that opened in the city and not a woman at all."

Fearing he could be right, she stared at her notes with frustration pounding at her temples. Her stomach rumbled loudly. Embarrassment heated her cheeks. Frosty lifted his head and placed his chin on her knee. She rubbed him behind the ears.

Carter frowned. "You need to eat." He stood and stretched. "Let's go. We can continue this tomorrow."

"I'd rather keep working," she said. Her life was on the line. They needed to figure out who and why someone was trying to kill her. "Can we order in?"

His parents had called to say they were taking Ellie to dinner and a movie, which meant she and Carter were on their own. The prospect of an intimate meal shared with Carter was both thrilling and unnerving.

"How about we go to Griffin's?"

The diner was an established neighborhood haunt and one of her favorite places located not far from the NYC K-9 Command Unit and her small apartment. The thought of seeing a friendly face or two appealed. She relented. "Sure."

He picked up the lead from the chair where he'd placed it when they'd entered the room and made a clucking sound with his mouth. Frosty rose and went to his side to be leashed up.

They left the building and Rachelle's breath caught in her throat when Carter snagged her elbow, pulling her close. He smelled good, masculine and musky, and his protectiveness made her feel special. Which was ridiculous.

She wasn't special. He was doing his job, nothing more.

They stepped through the diner's door and the aromas of savory dishes had her tummy cramping and her mouth watering.

"Well, look who's here! Our own Georgia peach!" Lou Griffin's loud voice boomed as he came out from behind the counter.

Glad to be out of the August humidity, Rachelle broke away from Carter and Frosty with a grin as she headed over to give the older gentleman a hug. "Hey, Lou."

Extracting herself from Lou's bear hug, she looked past the new appliances, gleaming counters and filled tables of the main diner to the area in the back they called the Dog House. An area designated for NYPD K-9 officers to eat while providing a place of rest for their canine partners.

The walls were covered with pictures to honor fallen officers. Rachelle's attention caught immediately on the newest photo that had been added to the display—Jordan Jameson.

She really wanted to invade that sacred space, to question the other officers and get their take on Jordan's murder, but she knew her questions wouldn't be welcome. More to the point, *she* wouldn't be welcome. At least not on her own. But if Carter invited her—though there was no way he would allow her to ask anyone about his brother.

Carter shook Lou's hand and commented, "If I didn't know, I'd never guess you had a fire here."

More specifically, a bomb. Rachelle shuddered to think what could have happened if K-9 officers Gavin Sutherland and Brianne Hayes hadn't been eating in the diner that night and if their dogs hadn't alerted, allowing the two officers to evacuate everyone from the building.

Because she knew the owners and had been there the night of the explosion, she had made a case to her boss that she should write an article about the bombing and the arrest of both the bomber and the real estate developer who was behind the destruction in an attempt to force Griffin's out for gentrification of the neighborhood. But her boss had assigned the story to a more "seasoned" male counterpart. She knew she shouldn't let the twist of frustration deep in her chest change her, but she woke with it every morning and she hadn't been able to let the story go.

Barbara Griffin walked out of the back tying an apron around her waist. "The remodelers did a really good job, didn't they?" She opened her arms.

Rachelle moved in for a hug. The Griffins

had appointed themselves as the welcome committee for this transplanted Georgia girl.

Barbara released Rachelle, then gave Carter a hug. "It's been a long time since we've seen you here."

"I know," he said, his gaze straying to the Dog House wall.

Patting his arm with obvious sympathy, she said, "Violet's working on a grand reopening celebration. I hope you both will attend."

Violet was their adult daughter who helped run the diner when she wasn't working at the customer service desk at LaGuardia Airport. She had recently married Carter's brother, K-9 Officer Zach Jameson, in a small wedding that was attended only by family and close friends. Rachelle had to admit to a spurt of envy for Violet and Katie. To be welcomed into the Jameson family, to feel their love and support, would be a dream come true.

Good thing she'd learned that dreams and reality rarely coincided.

"Of course I will attend the grand opening," Rachelle assured Barbara, touched by the invitation. The perfect opportunity for her to do a follow-up story that her boss couldn't refuse. "I'll even do a write-up about it for the paper."

"We will not be pushed out by gentrification," Lou heatedly vowed. "You can print that."

Barbara put a hand on his arm. "Don't get yourself worked up again, dear."

He covered her hand. The obvious love they shared made Rachelle ache in a strange way. She'd never seen her own parents display genuine affection for one another. Nor had she experienced it herself.

"I know, I know," Lou said. "Think of sailing calm waters on a balmy day. *Relax*." He drew the last word out.

Barbara went up on tiptoe to give her husband a peck on the cheek. "Exactly."

Carter looked at Rachelle. "Do you want to eat here or get dinner to go?"

Knowing this might be her only opportunity to sit in the Dog House, she said, trying not to sound too eager, "Here."

"Sounds good. Let's go get a table."

"I'll meet you back there. I need to wash my hands," she told him.

Carter and Frosty walked into the back section.

When they were out of earshot, Barbara sidled up to Rachelle. "Oh, what's going on here? You and the handsome officer? Do tell."

A heated flush rose up Rachelle's neck. "No, we're not... Our—" She hesitated to call what they had a relationship. "We're working on something together. Professionally."

Lou went behind the counter. "The way he was watching you, I'd say he has more than a professional interest in you."

With her heart fluttering at the suggestion that Carter felt anything more than duty toward her, she shook her head. "It's really not like that. We've only just met."

"Carter deserves some happiness," Barbara observed. "It was tragic the way his wife died. It's past time for him to find love again."

Not sure how to respond to her statement, Rachelle excused herself and hurried to the restroom. She put some cool water on her face, but nothing could calm the secret yearning to be more to Carter than a burden from taking root inside of her.

She'd never considered herself one to willingly take on heartache but that was exactly what would happen if she allowed herself to hope there was a chance at a future with the handsome Jameson brother.

Slapping a hand to her forehead, she told herself, *Get a grip. Stay focused.* Staying alive and furthering her career were the priorities. Not romance. And certainly not with a man who had made it clear she was a temporary fixture in his life.

Girding her emotions behind a well-constructed wall, she entered the Dog House portion of the restaurant and scanned the busy room. There were many tables with officers of various ranks. Carter had taken a seat at a table near the back with three officers. Frosty was in the porch area with several other dogs.

Carter waved her over. As she approached, she was aware of the curious glances of everyone in the room. She was a stranger entering a strange land. Nervous flutters had her tummy jumping as she slid into a seat beside Carter.

A female officer with auburn hair and big brown eyes smiled at her. "Carter was just telling us about you. I'm sorry to hear you've had a rough time of it lately. But you're in good hands with Carter." She held out her hand. "I'm Brianne Hayes."

"Nice to meet you." Rachelle shook the woman's hand. "Thank you. Carter's been great. Very protective."

A speculative gleam entered her gaze. "I would hope so." She gestured to the man next to her. "This is Gavin Sutherland."

He reached across Brianne to shake Rachelle's hand. "Welcome." As he settled his arm around Brianne in a way that made it clear they were couple, he said, "Carter mentioned you're a reporter."

Rachelle braced herself for the disdain she was sure would come. "I am. For *NYC Weekly*."

"I've seen you in the diner." The third officer, a big man with brown hair and hard features, eyed her warily with his dark brown gaze. "No comment."

Tucking in her chin, Rachelle said, "Okay."

"Knock it off, Tony," Carter said with a smile. "She's off duty." He turned his blue eyes on her. "Right?"

"Right. Except…" She smiled at him. "I am writing an article about you and the police dog field trials so…" She looked around the table. "I'd love to include anything you all could tell me about the competition."

Tony sat back and pointed a finger at Carter. "He and Frosty will win."

"I'll be happy to place," Carter said. "There's some stiff competition this year. I've been hearing good things about the team from Boston PD."

"Is anyone else from the command unit competing?" Rachelle asked.

"Are Luke and Bruno running the course this year?" Brianne asked.

Carter looked thoughtful. "I believe so."

Barbara came over to take their orders. Rachelle ordered the daily special of Atlantic salmon over rice and mixed vegetables. Carter went for the meat loaf plate.

The conversation turned to politics, which

created a lively debate on several issues facing the NYPD.

"You're not from New York," Brianne observed. "I detect a Southern accent."

"You're correct," Rachelle admitted. "Georgia."

"Tell us about home," Gavin said. "I've been to Florida."

Rachelle laughed. "Not exactly the same sort of Southern." She told them of growing up in the onion capital of the US. "In the spring we have a world famous Onion festival."

"What does one do at an onion festival?" Carter asked.

"It's a big deal. The festival is shown on the Food Network and all sorts of culinary events take place showcasing the sweet onion. There's a carnival and concerts with some big name country artists, a Little Miss Onion pageant for the up-to-twelve-year-olds. A Teen Onion and Miss Onion pageant. A parade—"

"And which year did you win?" Carter's teasing tone sent a ripple of laughter through his friends.

A blush crept up her neck. "What makes you think I entered?"

His eyebrows dipped together. "You didn't?"

"I did," she said, and hated how her voice sounded defensive. "I won when I was ten."

"Ah." He gave her a smug smile. "I knew it."

"And again when I was fourteen."

Tony let out a soft whistle. "Whew. We're in the presence of royalty."

Carter grinned. "Two wins. Good for you."

She sighed. Embarrassment curled her toes within her shoes. "Actually, I won again when I was seventeen."

"Nice," Brianne said. "Way to go."

Her face flamed. She was sure they thought she was as vain as they came. She didn't mention that her mother had pressured her to enter each time. And hoping to gain her approval, Rachelle had complied only to be disappointed when her mother still found fault with her even after being crowned.

Hoping to steer the conversation away from the pageant, she said, "The other claim to fame we have is the Vidalia onion was an answer on *Jeopardy.*"

Barbara arrived with their orders, stalling any more conversation about her hometown. Instead, as they ate, the officers talked shop and she was content to listen, absorbing the nuances of their speech and the shorthand language they used.

Lou came over to clear their plates. "Dessert?"

"Apple pie for me," she told him. "No ice cream."

"Me, too." Brianne said. "With an extra scoop of ice cream."

"I'll have the same," Gavin said.

"Not me," Tony said. "I need to head out." He rose and nodded to Rachelle. "Nice to meet you." He took his dinner ticket to the cashier station to pay Barbara.

"Can I have a bite of your pie?" Carter asked Rachelle. "I don't want a whole piece of my own."

Surprised and pleased, she nodded. "Of course."

When Lou brought the slices of pie, he handed Carter an extra fork.

Sharing the warm gooey pie with Carter, Rachelle told herself not to read too much into the gesture. It was only pie they were sharing, not their hearts.

After their desserts, Rachelle said goodbye to her new friends and then fell into step with Carter and Frosty and headed for the exit. She'd enjoyed meeting the officers and learning more about them as individuals and as a team. "My dinner was delicious."

"Agreed. Barbara's meat loaf is almost as good as my mom's," Carter said, placing his hand at the small of her back as they stepped outside. While still light out, twilight was approaching and the heat and humidity from earlier in the day had eased considerably.

"You know, it's funny that you and I hadn't

met before the other day," he said. "You seem to be very close to the Griffins."

"They've been very good to me. I'd seen you in the Dog House with your brothers and the other officers," she told him. "But as a civilian, I never dared venture into that part of the diner."

"Ah. I guess I wasn't paying very good attention." He guided her around the K-9 Unit building to the back, where he'd parked his vehicle.

She wasn't sure how to take his words. Was he saying he was remiss in not noticing her? The thought was thrilling.

Once they were safely inside the vehicle, she let out a breath that eased the constriction in her chest. She hadn't realized how the tension of the day had tightened her nerves and irritated her already-sore muscles. Even being in the coveted inner sanctuary of the Dog House, surrounded by a dozen other officers, hadn't set her mind at ease.

"I've been thinking," she said as he started the engine.

"Uh-oh. That could be trouble."

"What?"

The corners of his mouth tipped upward. He was teasing her.

Warmth spread through her. "What if the name Ophelia isn't a woman or a restaurant, but a boat?"

His eyebrows rose. "A boat?"

"Yeah. Lou mentioned sailing calm waters and it occurs to me that many boats have a female name. One of the photos I found on his social media was of him on a boat, remember?"

"You could be onto something there." The approval in his tone tickled her. "Tomorrow we'll search for any registered boats with the name Ophelia."

"Or we could take a quick detour to the World's Fair Marina in Flushing Bay. See if we can spot a vessel with that name."

"Trouble with a capital *T*," he stated. "No."

"We wouldn't even have to get out of the vehicle," she told him. "Just drive through the marina. Nothing dangerous about having a look."

"Every moment with you is dangerous," he muttered beneath his breath.

Obviously he didn't like having to protect her. "I'm sorry I've been such a bother." She crossed her arms and looked out the side window. "I would think you'd want to do everything possible to find your brother's killer."

"You're not a bother," he said. "And I do."

She turned to face him again. "Then let's check out the marina."

He drummed his fingers on the steering wheel. "What makes you think Miles owns the boat?"

"The picture, remember? I could totally be off base but it would be worth the time and effort to see. We have nothing to lose if I'm wrong."

"Why the World's Fair Marina?"

"It's the closest marina to the warehouse owned by Miles in Flushing," she replied.

She watched his internal debate play across his handsome face.

"Ellie's with your parents," she offered. "We don't have to rush home."

Her automatic urge to refer to his family's property as home made her ache with a yearning she wasn't willing to consider.

"I guess it wouldn't do any harm," he said, albeit grudgingly.

"Thank you." She settled back with satisfaction. They were doing something proactive. As a team. And she'd be grateful for however long it lasted.

Carter pulled the vehicle to the curb near the gate leading to the docks of the World's Fair Marina just as the sun set, casting long shadows across the water of Flushing Bay. Lampposts shone a warm glow over the various-sized boats tied to cleats on the dock. All appeared quiet. Except at the far left side of the marina, a light was out. Unease slithered up his spine and settled at the base of his neck.

"We'll have to come back," he said. "The gate has a keyless entry."

Popping the passenger door open, she said, "Let's get a little closer." She hopped out and shut the door.

"Hey!" *Unbelievable.* Irritation mingled with dread as Carter scrambled from the vehicle. He quickly released Frosty, leashed him up and hustled after Rachelle. "You promised you'd stay in the car."

"I made no such promise," she drawled, giving him an affronted look. "I said we wouldn't have to get out. But I didn't promise I would stay in the car."

He pinched the bridge of his nose where a headache was brewing. "Semantics."

"No, not semantics." She put a hand over her heart. "I never break my promises."

She sounded so sincere he had trouble hanging on to his annoyance. "Whatever. We need to leave."

"We have to get in there." She turned away to inspect the gate.

"I'm not climbing over the fence and neither are you."

She sighed and started walking along the fence line. "I wish I had binoculars. I can't see the names." She halted. "Wait there's one called

Riptide. Do you know that I've never actually been out on a boat?"

Carter shook his head. "You are an interesting woman."

"I imagine you say that to all the girls." She gave him a cheeky smile.

"No. I don't."

She titled her head and studied him for a moment before quickly looking away. "There's a streetlight out at the other end of the dock."

He'd been hoping she wouldn't notice. But he had a feeling she noticed everything. "Not much we can do about it tonight. Let's go."

"Wait." She shrugged off his hand. "There are people out there."

He squinted and, sure enough, he saw movement. Acid churned in his stomach. Nothing good could be happening in the dark in such an isolated place. He needed to get her out of there.

"Don't you want to check it out?"

"I don't have a warrant or probable cause. A burned-out light is not enough."

A low growl emanated from Frosty's throat and then a series of alerting barks. Carter spun around and noticed two men coming toward them. One had a bandage over his nose and the other a bandage around his forearm.

The men who'd tried to abduct Rachelle.

Had they followed them to the marina?
Alarm pulsed through Carter.
One of the men held a gun.

NINE

"Halt!" Carter yelled. "Police."

The man with the gun aimed at them.

Fearing for Rachelle's safety, Carter snagged an arm around her waist and pulled her down behind a metal garbage container just as shots rang out and bullets pinged off the metal. He reeled in Frosty's lead, tucking the dog close.

Pulse pounding in his ears, he unholstered his weapon and peered around the edge of the garbage container as he radioed for backup.

The two men ran to the gate and entered the code into the keyless lock. The gate opened, and they ran through and along the docks toward the darkened corner. The guy with the gun continued to fire off random shots at them.

"Carter, you have to go after them," Rachelle said.

"I'm not leaving you."

An engine roared to life. Carter jumped to his feet in time to see a lighted boat speeding away from the dock. Carter took out his cell phone and snapped off pictures. He doubted the photos would be any help, but he had to do something.

He called the situation in on the radio attached to his shoulder as they hurried back to his vehicle. And he asked for the harbor patrol to search for the boat. Though he knew by the time the patrol got out on the water, the escaped vessel could be miles away in a multitude of directions.

Hustling Rachelle to his vehicle parked at the curb, Carter glimpsed a white van parked in a far corner of the lot. The same van used by the men who'd tried to kidnap Rachelle earlier.

As they waited inside the vehicle, Carter said, "You know, I'm going to catch flak for bringing you here."

"Surely your brother can't get mad at you for following a clue."

"Oh yes, he can."

And he was proved correct a short time later when Noah climbed out of his K-9 Unit vehicle with his dog, Scotty, a majestic rottweiler trained for emergency service work. Along with Noah was Gavin Sutherland and his dog, Tommy, a springer spaniel who excelled at bomb detection. After instructing Gavin and Tommy to check out the van, Noah and Scotty headed to where Carter, Rachelle and Frosty waited by the curb.

The disgruntled expression on his brother's face didn't bode well. "What are you two doing down here?"

"Following a hunch," Carter said.

"It's my fault," Rachelle said. "I talked Carter into coming down here to search for a boat named *Ophelia.*"

Carter stared at her. Why would she try to protect him from Noah? A strange sort of pleasure infused him and made him stand taller.

Noah arched an eyebrow. "I doubt, Miss Clark, that you could talk my brother into anything he didn't want to do. I know I have not been able to over the years." Noah shifted his attention to Carter. "So tell me, brother, how did you come across this lead?"

"It wasn't my clue," Carter told him. "It was Rachelle's. She figured it out." Carter smiled encouragingly at Rachelle. "Go ahead, tell him."

She blinked, clearly surprised and pleased. For some reason pleasing her filled his chest with warmth and tenderness.

"I was scouring Miles's social media sites. And I found a reference to the name Ophelia. I thought maybe an old girlfriend or employee. But we had no luck tracking down a woman by that name. But then I thought maybe the name belonged to a boat. I came across a photo of Miles on one, so it stood to reason…"

"As it turns out," Carter said, "she was right."

He showed his brother the photo of the retreating vessel. Though the image was blurry, they could make out the name painted in blue letters across the back—*Ophelia.*

"All clear," Officer Gavin Sutherland called. "Tommy didn't alert."

Tommy was an excellent bomb detection dog and Carter trusted the canine's nose. Carter let out a relieved breath. He hadn't expected there to be an explosive in the van, but one never knew. It was best to be prepared.

Noah donned latex gloves and opened the side panel door. Carter tugged Rachelle behind him just in case there were any surprises waiting inside.

The van was empty. There were splashes of blood inside the cargo hold and on the door frame. From where Frosty had bitten one thug and Rachelle had broken the nose of the other.

Frosty strained at the end of his lead.

Noah nodded. "Let's see what he can find."

Carter dropped the lead and Frosty jumped into the back of the van. He sniffed around and then let out a bark.

"He's found something," Carter said, leaning

inside, careful not to touch anything. "I can see brass under the passenger seat."

"All right, everyone step back," Noah instructed. "I'll have our forensic team scour the van for evidence."

Once Carter had Frosty back in control, Rachelle asked, "Brass?"

"Unspent bullet," he clarified.

"You two head home. We've got this," Noah said.

Carter heard Rachelle's little humph of frustration. He felt the same way.

"We'd like to stay," Carter said. "These men tried to kidnap her today and shot at us. I want to know what they're up to and how this relates to—" He stopped himself from saying Jordan's name. His gaze flicked to Gavin and back to his brother.

Noah gave a slow nod. "Understood. Fine. Stay back."

Carter ushered Rachelle and Frosty away from the van and stopped a few feet away.

Rachelle slipped her hand into Carter's. "Thank you."

The place where their palms pressed together created a firestorm engulfing his arm and heading for his chest. "For what?"

"Everything."

He wasn't sure he deserved thanks. He'd only been doing his duty.

As they waited for the forensic team, he was achingly aware of Rachelle, her fingers flexed around his and her lavender scent teasing his senses. He saw the curious and speculative glances of his brother and Gavin but chose to ignore them.

When the forensic team was done, Noah walked over. His gaze flicked to where Carter still held Rachelle's hand. For a split second Carter thought of retracting his hand from Rachelle's but then dismissed the idea.

He liked holding her hand; he liked the connection.

He met Noah's steely gaze, daring him to say something. No doubt he'd get an earful from his brother later about keeping a firm line between work and personal feelings. Carter had never had trouble keeping an emotional barrier between him and, well, everyone else. But this woman was slowly, methodically, undermining his walls.

But guilt was piling on fast. Reminding him he couldn't let himself feel anything. He owed it to Helen not to give his heart away again. Carter loosened his hold on Rachelle, but she tightened hers, keeping his hand trapped within her grasp.

Noah's mouth quirked at the corner. He shook

his head and then cleared his throat. "The forensic team found a high-caliber bullet underneath the front seat. No fingerprints."

"What about the blood?" Carter asked.

"We'll type it," Ilana Hawkins, one of the forensic techs, said as she paused next to Noah. "Not sure it will lead anywhere but if our suspects have DNA in any database, then we'll be able to ID them."

"Thank you, Ilana. Good work," Noah said.

She smiled and walked to where the other two techs waited by their mobile forensic unit vehicle.

"Now what?" Rachelle asked. "Do you raid Miles's warehouse?"

"I can make a case with the commissioner to get a warrant," Noah said. "I've got people sitting on the warehouse. There's been no activity in the past twenty-four hours."

"He must have other property," Rachelle said. "We need to get back to the station and get back to work."

"Not tonight," Carter told her. "We're done for now. Tomorrow we can keep searching."

"But—"

He squeezed her hand. "No. I want to see my daughter."

Rachelle's eyes grew wide. "Oh, of course. Forgive me. Yes, let's go home."

"We'll see you there." Noah's chuckle rankled.

Carter tugged his hand free of Rachelle's and narrowed his gaze on Noah. "Not a word."

If Noah blabbed to their parents that Carter and Rachelle had stood holding hands like a couple, Carter would never hear the end of it.

Noah held up his hands in mock surrender. "I have no idea what you're talking about."

Shaking his head, Carter led the way to his vehicle. When they arrived back at the house Carter was able to park at the curb in front. He used his house key to open his parents' front door. "Hello."

The sound of pounding feet echoed through the house. Ellie tore out of the living room, followed closely by his mother and father. And two little yipping puppies.

"You came back!" Ellie cried and launched yourself into Rachelle's arms and hugging her tight.

Carter's jaw dropped. *Seriously?*

Over Ellie's head, Carter met Rachelle's surprised gaze. His insides twisted. He wanted to be the center of his daughter's world. If that made him selfish, then so be it. "Hey, what about me?"

Ellie wiggled out of Rachelle's arms and threw herself against Carter. "Daddy!"

He picked her up and held on tight, relishing the feel of his precious child.

The puppies nipped at Rachelle's pants. Laughing, she got down on the floor to shower the two miscreants with snuggles and praise. Frosty even edged his way in to lick her face. Her laughter was infectious. Carter's heart squeezed tight.

Giggling, Ellie shimmied out of his arms to join the lovefest on the floor. She pushed her way onto Rachelle's lap and joined in the fun with the puppies and Frosty, who now lay down with his paws on Rachelle's knee. The sight, so achingly sweet and tender, was almost more than Carter could bear.

And he found himself jealous of his daughter, the puppies and Frosty as Rachelle lavished her affection and attention so easily on them. He wanted it for himself. Which made no sense at all.

He tore his gaze away and found his parents watching the scene with bemused smiles. Carter had to put a stop to this now. Everyone was getting too close, too attached, too emotional.

He clapped his hands to gain everyone's attention. A trick he'd learned from Ellie's preschool teacher. "All right. It's time for a bath and bedtime stories."

Ellie leaned back into Rachelle's arms. "Can Rachelle read my bedtime stories to me tonight?"

Carter's stomach sank. Way too attached. "Honey, it's been a really long day, and I would really like to spend some time with you."

"Your father's right. It's been a very long day." She stifled a yawn. "I can read to you another time."

Grateful for her assist, Carter bent to pick Ellie up into his arms and then held out a hand to help Rachelle to her feet.

For a moment she clung to him. And he had the strangest sensation that if he could allow it, they could be a family.

Jolted by the thought, he quickly disengaged and stepped away from Rachelle. "We'll see you in the morning." He set Ellie on her feet. "Give Grandma and Grandpa kisses and thank them for your special day."

She ran to her grandparents and gave them noisy kisses. "Thank you, Grandma and Grandpa."

Ellie then raced back to Rachelle and wrapped her arms around her legs. "You'll still be here tomorrow, right?"

Rachelle rubbed Ellie's back. "I believe I will be. Now off with you. Sweet dreams."

Carter grabbed a puppy under each arm. "Ellie, get the door, please. Come on, Frosty. 'Night, Mom, Dad."

Ellie opened the front door so Carter and Frosty could pass through. As she shut the door, Carter heard Ellie say, "Sweet dreams to you, too, Rachelle."

The next morning Rachelle awoke to the smell of bacon and coffee. Hungry and eager to start the day, she quickly dressed in navy capris and a flowered top that had flounces at the elbows and the neckline. The top was feminine and made her feel pretty. And she had to admit to herself that she wanted to look pretty and hoped that Carter noticed.

"Really?" she asked her reflection in the bathroom mirror as she plaited her hair into a single braid down her back because the heat index was to reach triple digits. "What do you hope will happen? Carter will declare his undying love for you? Ha!" Shaking her finger at herself, she said, "Don't get all gooey about Carter. You are not looking for romance."

They were only together to solve a crime and keep her alive. With a shudder, she really hoped and prayed that today would not be a repeat of yesterday. Nearly being kidnapped and shot at had never been on her bucket list. In fact, none of this had been on her bucket list.

When she'd decided to write an investigative

piece on Jordan Jameson's murder she never dreamed she would become a target herself or that she would end up ensconced deep within the Jameson clan.

Or find herself longing for Carter Jameson.

Frustrated with herself, she stuffed those feelings deep inside. There was no room in her life for emotions that had no place to grow. Carter wasn't interested in her romantically and once her life was back to normal, she'd probably never see Carter or his adorable daughter again. The thought saddened her more than she wanted to admit.

When she stepped into the kitchen, Carter and Ellie were at the counter eating bacon, pancakes, fresh berries and drinking orange juice. Through the window in the back door, Rachelle could see Alex Jameson in the backyard with the puppies. Frosty lay on the porch observing. She assumed Scotty had gone with Noah to the NYC K-9 Command Unit headquarters.

"Good morning," Rachelle said.

Carter smiled. "Ellie wanted to see you. So we came down for breakfast."

Touched, Rachelle hugged the child. Ellie gave her a sweet kiss on the cheek.

Ivy Jameson handed her a cup of coffee. "Milk?"

"No, thank you. You wouldn't by chance have an alternative creamer?"

"Let me check the cupboard. I usually keep a variety of things here for when we host Bible study." She pulled out a powdered nondairy creamer. "Will this work?"

Rachelle would've preferred an almond beverage, but she took the nondairy creamer. "Thank you so much." She applied a liberal amount to her coffee and stirred with the spoon Ivy handed her.

"Sit here." Ellie patted the bar stool beside her. "I'm going with my friend Greta and her mom to Prospector Park."

"Prospect Park," Carter corrected.

Taking a seat, Rachelle said, "I've never been there. Is it an outdoor playground?"

"It's one of the biggest parks in the five boroughs," Carter told her. "With lots of shade trees."

"I'm sure you will have lots of fun, Ellie." Rachelle skipped the pancakes but took a spoonful of berries and several pieces of bacon, which she doused with syrup.

"Do you not like pancakes?" Ellie asked.

Rachelle shook her head. "Not really. But I love bacon."

Carter's soft chuckle heated her cheeks. "A little bacon with your syrup?"

She grimaced. "I wasn't allowed much in the way of sweets as a kid so now I go a little overboard."

He cocked his head and looked like he wanted to ask questions. Hoping to keep him from delving into her childhood, she stuffed her mouth. Thankfully, he let her comment go.

After breakfast, Rachelle helped Ivy with the dishes while Carter and Ellie went to their apartment so Ellie could get ready for her outing with her friend.

"Thank you, my dear," Ivy said. "Carter told us what happened to you yesterday." Concern laced her words. "Despite my initial reaction to your occupation, I hope you know you're welcome to stay here with us as long as you need. Between Alex and Carter and Noah and the dogs, we will keep you safe."

Touched to the point of tears, Rachelle blinked rapidly and busied herself drying the dish in her hand. "I really appreciate your offer."

And she did, more than Mrs. Jameson could ever know. She felt wanted here, like she belonged. She knew she was getting herself in too deep, emotionally. She really needed to take a step back. But that time would come eventually. And it would hurt, but until then she would enjoy the sense of family, of belonging.

"Are you ready to go?" Carter stepped into the kitchen a few minutes later.

Drying her hands off on the dish towel, Rachelle nodded. "Yes." She was eager to get digging more into Miles Landau's life. "Thank you, Ivy, for breakfast."

"My pleasure," the older woman said. She turned to Carter. "Keep her safe."

A flash of surprise in Carter's eyes turned to determination. "Of course."

When they arrived at the station, there was a buzz of activity going on. Carter led her to the conference room. "I'll be right back. I'm going to see what's happening."

He shut the door behind her. Wondering if there was news regarding Jordan's case, Rachelle immediately went to work looking for something that would lead them to Miles.

An hour later Carter returned just as she was getting up to go look for him to share what she'd found.

"Everything okay?"

"Yes. The August heat brings out the crazy in everybody." He ran his hand through his thick dark hair. Her gaze tracked his movement and her fingers curled against the itch to feel his hair, to brush back the stray lock that fell over his forehead. "There was some gang activity and a robbery. Nothing unusual."

Forcing herself to focus, she said, "I think I found something that might be useful."

He crossed the room to her side with purposeful strides. "Show me."

"I was reading through all the comments on Miles's Facebook page. He has quite the list of friends and followers. Anyway, this is from a couple of days after his release from prison."

She showed him the post. It was a picture of Miles mugging for the camera outside the prison. His shaved head gleamed like a recently polished bowling ball. His thin frame was muscled and his dark eyes had a feral light. The caption accompanying the photo read, *Watch out, here I come.*

"Ominous but not a direct threat to anyone in particular," Carter said.

"This is what I wanted to show you." She scrolled down through the two hundred-plus comments and landed on one that read, *Looking forward to you coming home.*

"Who is that from?"

"Cecilia Landau," she said. "I checked out her social media pages and I believe she's Miles's mother. He might be hiding out at her place."

"That is a good catch."

Approval resonated in his tone and pleasure infused her.

"I'll let Noah know and he should send officers over." He headed for the door.

"Wait."

Carter stopped and arched an eyebrow.

"You and I should go over. She might talk to me."

He shook his head. "No way. I'm not putting you back out in the field. After what happened last night…"

"But you and Frosty would be with me," she argued. "Though I would suggest putting on civilian clothes." She gestured to his uniform. "Less intimidating that way."

"Noah will never go for it."

She hurried to his side. "We won't know unless we ask him."

"Suit yourself." He gestured for her to precede him out of the conference room.

Carter rapped on Noah's door, then opened it so she could pass through first. She really liked the way Carter was so polite and thoughtful.

Despite the nervous flutter in her tummy, she told Noah what she'd found and what she'd like to do. Even before she finished he was shaking his head.

Frustration ate a hole through her patience. "Listen, both of you. I appreciate that you're trying to protect me but if we don't find Miles this will never end. Mrs. Landau is not going to willingly talk to the police—I can guarantee you that. But she might talk to me. If I come at her saying I'm doing a report on recently released inmates and want to include her son, she might be more inclined to talk to me. Everyone wants their fifteen minutes of fame."

"It's too big a risk," Carter said. "If Miles is the one after you he would have told his mother about the nosy reporter."

"Maybe not," she countered. "She may be in the dark about his current activity."

Noah rubbed his chin. "We could bring Mrs. Landau in for questioning."

"Then she's guaranteed not to talk," Rachelle stated.

"I won't authorize a visit, it would be too risky, but a phone call couldn't do any harm," Noah said.

Forcing herself to be content with a call, Rachelle hurried back to the conference room to look up the number.

She would have to employ all of her charm to get Mrs. Landau to talk to her.

Rachelle was up to the task.

TEN

At the end of the day, Rachelle was discouraged. Mrs. Landau had hung up on her at the first mention of her son, Miles.

And though Rachelle and Carter had gone through every last scrap of her notes and research, they'd come up with nothing solid. No new leads on Jordan's killer.

She prayed the police caught Miles soon. Then they'd know one way or another if he was the murderer they sought.

When they arrived home to the three-story house in Rego Park, Ellie hadn't returned from her outing to the park. Carter went upstairs to his apartment to change out of his uniform.

Needing some downtime as well, Rachelle went to the spare bedroom in his parents' portion of the large multifamily home that had become hers for the past few nights. It was a nice, comfortable room, with a double-size mattress and decorated in sea-foam green and cream.

She wondered if at one time this had been one of the boys' bedroom. Maybe Carter's?

With a sigh, she decided she really needed to keep her mind off the too-handsome officer. Nothing would come of letting herself pine for him when he had repeatedly made it clear he wasn't interested.

Lying on the bed, she closed her eyes to rest. The bang of a door opening, then Ellie's sweet voice drew her out of the bedroom like a butterfly to a flower.

Rachelle hung back in the shadow of the hallway as she watched the Jamesons greet each other. Carter, now wearing jogging shorts and a T-shirt, swept his daughter into his arms and kissed her face. She giggled as he made raspberry sounds against her neck.

Rachelle's heart ached with love and longing for this family. But they would never be hers. Saddened and dismayed at the same time by the thought, she began to retreat, deciding it was time to distance herself. But Ellie spied her before she had taken two steps.

"Rachelle." Ellie broke away from her father and ran to Rachelle, giving her a warm hug.

"Well, hello there," Rachelle said, aware of Carter's gaze on her and his daughter. "Did you have a good time at the park?"

"I did." Ellie slipped her hand into Rachelle's

and drew her into the living room. "We had a picnic and Greta and I met some nice girls to play with. I even saw Snapper."

"What?!" Carter and his parents, who had joined them, all stared at the child.

Rachelle tucked in her chin. "Isn't Snapper...?"

"Uncle Jordan's partner," Ellie said. "I hugged him and told him he should come home with me." Sadness crossed her face. "But he ran away and no one else saw him. Greta's mom was upset when I told her about Snapper. She said I shouldn't touch dogs without permission from their owner. But Snapper is family."

"Ellie, are you sure it was Snapper?" Alex asked, his voice breaking slightly.

"It could have been a different German shepherd, Ellie," Carter said gently. "And Greta's mom is correct. You know better than to approach a dog without permission, and even then, only if I'm with you."

Ellie shook her head adamantly. "It was Snapper. He had on his black collar."

Carter exchanged a look of disbelief with his dad.

Snapper disappeared the day Jordan had died. If the dog were still alive... Rachelle knew this was momentous. "We should go to the park," she said to Carter.

"There's no *we*," he said. "You're not going anywhere." He looked at his father. "I'll call Noah on the way."

Alex nodded, already moving to the hall closet, where he grabbed two flashlights.

Carter squatted down in front of Ellie. "Sweetie, can you describe where in the park you were when you saw Snapper?"

She scrunched up her little nose. "We were in the funny trees. We pumped water into a trunk and played in the sand."

"Sounds like they were in Zucker Natural Exploration Area," Ivy said. "It's just off Nellie's Lawn in the northeast part of the park."

"Got it." He gave Ellie a hug.

"Are you going to bring Snapper home?" Ellie asked.

"I'm going to try." He stood and met Rachelle's gaze. "You'll stay put?"

Though he had reason to ask, the question rankled. "Yes. I'll keep Ellie occupied while we wait for you to come back."

He gave a sharp nod before leaving with Frosty and his father.

"Who would like to help me fix dinner?" Ivy asked, breaking the silence.

Rachelle immediately said, "I will." Anything to keep her mind off being left behind while Carter and his father went in search of Snapper.

"Me, too," Ellie cried.

"Great." Ivy headed to the kitchen. "I'll send Katie a text and ask if she'd like to come down. She wasn't feeling well earlier. She has been so tired. The pregnancy is really taking its toll."

Rachelle would imagine the death of her husband was more the culprit. Her heart hurt for this family and all they had suffered. She wished she could solve the crime. She didn't want to find the truth for herself anymore. She wanted it for Carter and his family.

"Do you think she really saw Snapper?" his father asked as Carter drove them to Prospect Park, located in the neighboring borough of Brooklyn.

Steeling himself against the hope in his father's voice, Carter said, "I don't know, Dad. We can pray so."

Taking out his phone, he called Noah and told him what was happening. "Dad and I are on our way there now."

"I'll join you," Noah said, and clicked off.

Carter didn't think Ellie would make up a story about something so important, though she was an imaginative child. If Snapper were out there, he would have come home, wouldn't he? There had been so many sightings over the past five months and every time it was either the wrong dog or just a fool's errand. But if Ellie really had seen Snapper, then they had to try to find him.

By the time Carter pulled to a stop along Flatbush Avenue, two other vehicles from the NYC K-9 Command Unit pulled up behind him. Noah and his dog, Scotty, got out of his SUV. Tony Knight and his dog, Rusty, a male chocolate Lab specializing in search and rescue, climbed out of the next vehicle.

Carter shook hands with Tony. The man had been Jordan's best friend growing up. "Glad to see you."

"I was in with Noah when you phoned," Tony said. "I will do anything to help bring Snapper home."

"I put the call out," Noah said. "There will be others arriving to help in the search. The park is over 500 acres. Snapper could be anywhere or not even in the park by now, but we have to try."

Alex grabbed Snapper's bed from the back seat where he'd placed it before leaving the house and held it out for the dogs to sniff. "I snagged this so the dogs could get Snapper's scent."

"Good thinking, Dad," Noah said.

After Scotty, Frosty and Rusty had taken a whiff, Carter said, "Dad, Frosty and I will take the Zucker Natural Exploration Area."

Noah nodded. "Tony and Rusty, head toward the zoo."

As Carter, Frosty and his dad set off, more police vehicles arrived. Carter was glad to have Noah coordinating their search effort.

With the beam of their flashlights bobbing through the dense woods, Carter and his dad called Snapper's name. Frosty picked up a scent. Encouraged, Carter let the dog lead him and his dad through the park toward the west side. Frosty left the wooded, grassy area and stopped at the one-way road that bordered the park. He whined, indicating he'd lost the scent.

Had Snapper been picked up in a car?

A few moments later, several other dog and handler teams emerged from the woods. Apparently all the dogs had picked up Snapper's scent but the trail went cold at the road.

Disappointed and discouraged, Carter feared they might never find Snapper.

Late Friday afternoon, Carter finished up some last-minute paperwork, stalling, really, because tonight was the celebrity ball Rachelle was covering for the newspaper. He wasn't looking forward to attending. He wasn't much for swanky shindigs. Give him a baseball stadium or dog park, he felt comfortable. The Metropolitan Museum of Art, not so much.

"Hey, shouldn't you be headed home?" Noah stopped by Carter's desk.

"Soon."

While Carter had resumed his duties, Rachelle had remained safely in his parents' house with Ellie and his mom and dad. Dad would protect them all.

Carter hated admitting to himself how much he looked forward to going home at the end of every shift, not only because his daughter would be waiting, but also Rachelle.

He liked the way Rachelle's brown eyes lit up when she saw him, though she'd quickly try to hide her reaction. Just as he hid his own joy at seeing her. He wanted to believe it was only the close proximity heating up emotions between them. Not something deeper. He couldn't do deeper.

He really needed something to break on Rachelle's case. The more time she spent with his family, the harder it would be for them all when she left.

"Still no news on Snapper?" Carter asked, hoping to deflect his brother.

Unfortunately, Snapper hadn't been found at Prospect Park or anywhere in the vicinity despite every law enforcement officer keeping an eye out for the dog. Though Carter had worked his normal shift patrolling the subway system, he'd taken a walk through the park on his own several times hoping to find Snapper. Ellie had seemed so certain.

Noah shook his head. "All we can do is pray Snapper will find his way home if he's still alive."

Carter clenched his fist at the thought. "Yes. I'm not… I don't—" Carter stalled out, searching for words to voice the anguish lodged in his chest.

Noah put his hand on Carter's shoulder. "I know. Me, too." For a moment they were silent. Grief snarled in Carter's chest and he lifted up a prayer to ask that Snapper really was alive and would come home. It would do them all so much good.

Squeezing his shoulder before releasing him, Noah said, "Very impressive article she wrote for the *NYC Weekly* newspaper about Snapper and the search for him. She has a real gift with words."

Pride for Rachelle swelled in Carter's chest. "She did a great job. She's a skilled writer." He'd been a bit leery when she told him about the article but when he'd read it before she turned the piece in, he'd wanted to hug her for her kind and compassionate way of asking the public for help while still maintaining the family's privacy.

Noah grinned. "And I'm sure she'll do just

as excellent a job reporting on tonight's event. Ellie has been talking nonstop for the last two days about this ball you and Rachelle are going to. I think it's great you're willing to escort her."

Carter snorted. "I can't very well let her go on her own and she's bound and determined to go."

"True. It's not like she's under house arrest. She could leave on her own if she chose to. She has to continue to do her job, after all."

The thought of Rachelle out from under his protection, vulnerable and alone, made Carter's insides twist.

"I heard Mom say the girls were going shopping today," Noah said.

"What?" Carter's spine stiffened. "She left the house?"

"Calm down, calm down." Noah put up a hand like a traffic officer. "They have a uniformed escort."

Carter wasn't placated.

"Plus, Dad's with them," Noah added. "You know he's not going to let anyone near the ladies."

Taking a breath to calm his racing pulse, Carter let some tension ease from his body. When it came to protection, their father was the best. And Carter trusted him. If Dad felt there was a threat he'd take action. Carter just wished they had a dog with them.

As if reading his thoughts, Noah said, "Plus, I had Dad take Scotty with them. It's good for my partner to get out and stretch his legs during the day, instead of being cooped up in the office while I'm pushing paper as the interim chief."

Carter wanted to hug his brother. Except they weren't the hugging sort. "Thanks, man. I appreciate it."

"Of course. You would do the same for me."

"You know it. And I've no doubt the commissioner will make you the permanent chief. There's no one better suited after—" Carter swallowed back the sharp stab of grief. "Jordy would be proud of you. As am I."

A flash of surprise, then acceptance and brotherly love shone in Noah's eyes. "Thank you." Noah cleared his throat. "You better get on home. You have a penguin suit to squeeze yourself into."

Chuckling at the reminder, Carter said, "I do. You think they'd let me bring Frosty if I put a bow tie around his neck?"

Noah laughed. "You're both on guard duty. I think you should."

Rachelle sat on a stool in the middle of the Jameson guest bathroom wearing a belted robe as Katie and Ellie fussed with her hair. She winced slightly when Ellie tugged a little too hard. But she bit her lip, refraining from saying anything.

Today had been one of her most treasured experiences. She and the Jameson women had spent hours looking for the perfect dress and shoes for her to wear tonight to the celebrity ball. Though they'd had Alex and another patrolman, along with a beautiful rottweiler dog named Scotty, as their escorts, Rachelle, Ellie, Katie and Ivy had giggled their way through several shops until they'd found success and Rachelle had purchased a new gown.

Rachelle had planned to wear her one good dress, a long, black tank style she wore with pearls. Nothing fancy, just serviceable. But Katie and Ellie had taken one look at it and declared the dress wouldn't do. So now there was a stunning red dress with lace overlaying silk hanging on the back of Rachelle's bedroom door and a pair of new sparkly sandals waiting to be worn. She'd put it on a credit card, deciding the expense was worth the price.

All the attention and pampering was overwhelming. She could be the heroine of her own Cinderella story.

Ivy walked into the bathroom and clapped her hands. "Oh my, you look lovely."

"They won't let me look," Rachelle complained with a smile.

"Almost there," Katie said around a mouthful of bobby pins.

"Just a few more flowers," Ellie said.

Rachelle had the sinking feeling she might look like a wood nymph when they were done. Ellie had insisted on putting baby roses in her hair.

Katie had done Rachelle's makeup, and again she hadn't let her take a peek.

"Okay," Katie said as she stepped back, holding her hand out for Ellie. The little girl skidded around Rachelle's knees with a big smile on her face. "It's time for you to take a look."

Rachelle stood up gingerly so as not to dislodge whatever they'd done with her hair. As she gazed in the mirror, she swallowed past the lump in her throat. Her makeup was dramatic, yet not heavy. And Katie and Ellie had done some sort of a fancy twist around the crown of her head and gathered her hair into a long ponytail going over her shoulder. Little red, baby roses were embedded in her hair along the twist with a few woven into the ponytail. The effect was stunning.

Tears burned the back of her eyes. She blinked rapidly so she didn't ruin her mascara. She turned to the others. "Thank you. I don't know what to say." She looked in the mirror again. "I barely recognize myself."

Katie and Ellie and Ivy beamed at her.

"Carter's upstairs getting ready," Ivy said.

"Let's get you dressed," Katie said.

They hustled Rachelle to her bedroom. As Rachelle slipped into the red dress, she felt compelled to say, "I've never had anything like this before."

"It's a striking dress," Katie said while zipping up the back.

"It is, but that's not what I mean." Rachelle faced her new friends. "This girl time. I can't express how special today has been." Her throat grew tight. "I was an only child. My mother wasn't the touchy-feely type."

Katie put a hand on her shoulder. "You're one of us now. No matter what happens going forward, you will always be our friend."

Choking back tears, Rachelle smiled. "Thank you. I really am so grateful to all of you for everything you've done for me over the past week."

Ellie clapped her hands. "I can't wait for Daddy to see you."

A knot of anxiety formed in Rachelle's tummy. Would Carter think she was pretty?

They heard Carter's deep voice talking with his father in the living room.

"I guess I should go." Rachelle smoothed a hand over the front of the gown.

"Wait," Katie said. She picked up a jewelry box she'd placed on the dresser. "This will complete the look." The box held a sparkly strand of crystals and a matching bracelet. "These aren't real. They were a gift and I never wear them, but they would look lovely on you."

"Thank you." Touched by the other woman's thoughtfulness, she turned so Katie could close the clasp on the necklace.

The Jameson women walked ahead of Rachelle, giving her a moment to collect herself. She picked up the little sparkly black bag Ivy had lent her, which now held her flowered notebook and pink pen, her ID and some cash. She took a deep breath and walked into the living room.

"Here comes the princess," Ellie announced with much fanfare.

Rachelle caught sight of Carter and her heart stuttered and then pounded. She'd thought him handsome in his uniform and his casual clothing but in the tux, *wow*. His dark hair had been styled back off his forehead and his jaw was clean-shaven. Sitting beside him, Frosty wore a black K-9 police vest and a black bow tie rested beneath his chin.

They made quite a picture.

Carter's blue eyes collided with hers. They were icy and unreadable. A flutter of uncertainty made her want to look away. Instead, she lifted her chin and smiled.

Carter bent down to give his daughter a kiss. "You can stay with Aunt Katie tonight. We'll be home late."

"Okay, Daddy." With her little hands, she turned his face back toward Rachelle. "Doesn't she look pretty?"

"Yes. Very pretty." His voice was devoid of any inflection.

Rachelle swallowed the hurt of his nonreaction. She didn't need his approval or appreciation. This night wasn't about them. This night was about her career. She had a job to do. He was just her bodyguard. And she would repeat the phrase to herself over and over again all night long.

ELEVEN

Carter's heartbeat was so fast in his chest he was surprised Rachelle didn't hear it as he escorted her up the red carpet at The Metropolitan Museum of Art. Cameras flashed. People *oohed* and *ahhed* over the guests arriving. He really didn't like all this pomp and circumstance. But it was part of the deal. And Rachelle deserved to be fawned over. She was gorgeous. The red dress fit her to perfection and made her warm brown eyes shine. The crown of roses on her head made him think of one of Ellie's fairy tales. Rachelle was indeed a princess.

Inside the famed art museum, they followed the crowd to The Charles Engelhard Court in the American Wing. Twinkle lights dangled from the ceiling of the glass-enclosed courtyard and danced off the stained-glass windows. At the far end of the courtyard, in front of a facade of the Bank Branch of the United States, a band had been set up, complete with a dance floor.

Amid the large marble and gold-plated American sculptures, linen-clad tables with gold-rimmed china and sparkling crystal stemware created an intimate feel for the myriad guests squeezing into the space.

Carter usually didn't suffer claustrophobia, but he was beginning to understand the feeling as he and Frosty trailed in Rachelle's wake. She appeared comfortable among New York and Hollywood's elite. She stopped to talk to women in stunning and sometimes awful gowns, jotting down names of designers and accessories that made his head spin. More than one man paused to admire Rachelle as she moved through the throng. Carter had never considered himself the jealous type but as the night wore on, he found himself wanting to push a few overly eager men off their feet for getting too chummy with Rachelle.

After the dinner of chicken smothered in sauce alongside rice and vegetables, the band struck up their first set and people moved to the dance floor. Tired of the small talk with those at their table, Carter settled Frosty near a statue away from the crowd, snagged Rachelle's hand and drew her to the dance floor.

They moved to the music, a classical piece that permeated the air and for a moment made

Carter feel as though they were the only two people on the dance floor.

Holding her close, he said against her ear, "How soon can we get out of here?"

She leaned back to look at him, her eyes sparking with amusement. "It took longer than I expected."

"What?"

"I figured you'd become bored much sooner."

"Not bored." *Just tired of sharing you with everyone.* The thought made him stumble.

He twirled her in a circle and then steered her away from the dance floor toward a side exit leading to an outside balcony. He let out a soft whistle; a moment later Frosty joined them, trotting along at Rachelle's side.

"I need some fresh air," Carter explained as they left the revelry of the celebrity ball behind them.

She stepped out of his arms to lean against the handrail. He wanted to pull her back into his embrace.

"It's a beautiful night," she commented, gazing up at the stars.

"You're beautiful." In the moonlight he could see the surprise in her eyes.

A slow smile, different than any other he'd seen on her face, appeared. "I didn't think you noticed."

"Oh, I noticed. So did every man here."

She shrugged. "I'm here to do a job. I don't matter to any of these people beyond getting their name in the paper."

"You matter to me. More than I care to admit." Before he could stop himself, he fingered the long strands of her hair draped over her shoulder. Silky, smooth and so pretty.

"Carter?"

His name on her lips was like an elixir, taming the riot of emotions bouncing through him. "This thing between us can't go anywhere." The words were directed more at himself than her.

She stepped closer. "Why?"

"I'm not prepared to replace—" His chest hurt with grief. "I care for you, Rachelle. But I'm not free to—I can't offer you my heart." He hated to be so blunt, but he had to make sure she understood. He needed to keep his heart safe. He couldn't imagine going through the kind of pain he'd experienced when Helen died. Better not to love again than risk heartache.

She breathed in and slowly exhaled. "I understand. But we have this moment in time. It may be all we'll ever have."

The deep, honey tone of her Southern voice spread through him, overrunning his walls and making him believe her words. Giving in to the yearning for closeness, he cupped her face and lowered his lips to hers to kiss her the way he'd wanted since the moment he'd held her in his arms after her near miss with the subway train.

Rachelle couldn't breathe. But who needed air with Carter kissing her, curling her toes inside her little strappy sandals. Only this moment on the museum's ballroom balcony mattered. She clutched at the lapels of his tux to keep from melting into a puddle at his feet. A sense of rightness, of belonging, of being noticed, filled her every cell.

When they broke apart, they were both breathing rapidly as he touched his forehead to hers.

"Wow." His voice was husky and deep as if he, too, was having trouble catching his breath.

"Hmm, yes," she murmured, wanting so badly to repeat the experience but too shy to initiate another kiss.

He took a breath and lifted his head. "I didn't mean—"

A flood of embarrassment and irritation chased away her shyness. She stepped back and put a finger to his lips. "Don't you dare say you didn't mean to kiss me. Because I hope you did mean to, if only this once."

One corner of his mouth lifted in a salty grin. "Oh, I meant to kiss you. I've been wanting to for a long time."

For a long moment, he held her gaze and she was lost in the swirling blue depths. Then his grin faded, and his eyes seemed to cool. He disengaged from her. "This can't happen again. I can't allow anything to develop between us. I can't do that to Ellie, and I can't betray the memory of my wife."

Stricken to the core, she clapped her hands together in front of her. Suddenly the mild evening air was cold against her bare arms. "Of course."

He was still in love with his late wife. She could never compete with his memory of her. She lifted her shoulder in hopes to downplay the hurt spreading through her. "I understand."

She turned and hurried back inside the museum. She wandered aimlessly through the crowd, a smile plastered on her face. She needed to find the restroom or some little dark alcove where she could melt down in private. Or as private as it could get with over a hundred people milling about. Her lower lip trembled. She clenched her teeth together. She would not cry in public.

She headed for the far exit, where the restrooms were off to the right and the caterer's station off to the left. She passed the threshold into the hallway outside of the exhibit hall when a strong arm wrapped around her shoulders and something sharp poked in to her left side.

"Just keep walking," a deep voice said in her ear. "Or I'll gut you here. The boss doesn't want a scene. He wants you out of the way."

Her breath caught in her throat. She slanted a glance sideways. The tall man wore a waiter's jacket. His face was bruised around his nose and eyes. She swallowed as realization hit full force. This was one of the men who had tried to kidnap her the other day. The one whose nose she'd broken.

He steered her toward the catering doors. Horror filled her veins. If she let him take her through those shiny, swinging doors she was going to die.

Better to die here where there was a chance he would be caught. She had to do something. Cupping her left fist with her right hand, she took a deep breath and used as much force as she could muster to jab her elbow into his rib cage while at the same time she stomped down on his foot with her spiked heel.

He let out a foul curse, his hold on her lessening enough that she twisted away, running back toward the party. He grabbed the back of her dress and yanked her off her feet. She went down with a jolt onto the hard floor. Pain reverberated through her, stealing her breath.

A woman screamed.

Then she heard Carter's voice. "Attack!"

The scrabble of nails echoed on the marble floor and then the whirlwind of white fur flashed by as Frosty sprang at her attacker. Despite the agony pulsing through her body, she spun to face the assailant with her feet up and ready to defend herself. But she didn't need to. Frosty was standing on top of the man's chest, snarling and snapping his jaw.

"Hey! Get him off me!" The terrified man withered beneath Frosty.

Carter raced forward to kick the knife away. "Don't move or he'll bite."

The man froze.

Security guards and policemen rushed forward to take the man into custody. Carter called Frosty off so the man could be put in handcuffs and taken away.

Carter squatted down beside her and cupped her cheek. "Are you okay? Can you stand?"

"I'm just sore. Nothing broken." She hoped. She allowed him to help her to her feet. She tested her legs, her back and arms to reassure herself there were no broken bones.

Despite his earlier assertion that nothing could happen between them, she clung to him. He was her safeguard. Her anchor in this strange and violent storm.

And she knew there was no way she could fight her feelings for Carter. She could only hope she could hide them.

After giving their statements to the officers on scene, they were cleared to leave.

Carter handed her the little black purse she'd been carrying. He must have grabbed it from the table on his way to find her.

Going home sounded like an ideal plan. She had enough information to write her article about the fund-raiser and all the celebrities in attendance, and of course the part about being attacked by a rogue waiter would add drama, especially when she highlighted how a certain handsome officer and majestic white dog came to her rescue. She was still shaking from the scare. She sent up praise to God above for sending the pair to her aid when she needed them the most.

"He said the boss didn't want a scene. He wants me out of the way," she said. "Do you think Miles is his boss?"

"I'll find out when I question him," Carter replied as he guided her through the gathered crowd and toward the museum exit.

Carter called for a car to pick them up. They didn't have to wait long. They slid into the back and Rachelle leaned against the headrest, taking a few calming breaths.

Frosty lay curled on the floorboard. Carter had his face turned away from her as they traveled through the city.

She wanted Carter to hold her, but she wouldn't ask. If he didn't want to explore their growing attachment, then so be it. She had to learn to live within the parameters he'd set. She was used to craving love and affection and having it denied. There must be something wrong with her, that no one wanted to love her.

All the more reason to focus on her career.

The town car headed onto the Ed Koch Queensboro Bridge, taking the outer lane. From the side-view window Rachelle could see the borough of Queens laid out in yellow dots reflecting the night sky. Below the bridge lay the wide expanse of the East River.

The silence between them became too much for her to bear.

"Did you know the East River isn't really a river?" she asked Carter.

"No?"

She heard a hint of amusement in his tone but ignored it. "No. Despite its name it isn't truly a river but a saltwater tidal strait connecting Upper New York Bay with Long Island Sound."

"That is correct."

Definitely amused. "Did you know that water

of the strait flows in different directions depending on the time of day?"

"I think I remember learning something about that in school," he said drily.

She rolled her eyes at him even though it was too dark inside the car for him to notice. "I know you grew up here, but this is all new to me. The closest river near where I grew up, the Oconee River, provides drinking water for thousands of people in the state."

"You don't want to drink the East River water."

"I see people fishing in it."

"You don't want to do that, either. There are much better waterways to find good fish." He shifted to face her. "Do you fish?"

She shook her head. "My father took me fishing when I was young, much to my mother's dismay."

"Did you catch anything?"

"A cold," she confessed. "I wasn't patient enough to stand in the water with a pole, waiting for some wide-mouthed bass to bite."

"That sounds about right."

"What does that mean?"

"In the time I've known you I can say you aren't the type of person to sit idle for long."

True. She did like to keep busy. Either physically or mentally. "I don't see you relax much."

"Between the job, Frosty and Ellie, there's no time for relaxation."

"When was the last time you took a vacation?"

He rubbed his chin. "I took some time off when Ellie was born."

Her stomach clenched. Time to mourn his deceased wife. That didn't sound like a vacation. The man needed some downtime. For himself and for Ellie. "Have you considered taking Ellie to Disney World? I was about her age when my grandmother took me."

Though she couldn't make out his expression, she could feel his gaze on her in the shadowed interior of the car. "You still remember the trip?"

"Like it was yesterday." She reached across the seat to find his hand. "Take your daughter on a memorable trip. Let her dress up like a princess."

He gave her hand a squeeze. "I might do as you suggest."

The sound of a roaring engine filled the car's interior as harsh light shone in through the back window. Frosty lifted his head and growled.

From the front seat the driver said, "What's this guy doing?"

Rachelle sat up straight and glanced through the rear window and was momentarily blinded by multiple headlights on the large vehicle tailgating their car.

"He's awfully close," she said.

"Step on it," Carter told the driver. The car sped forward but so did the big truck behind them.

Carter grabbed his cell phone from the breast pocket of his tux jacket. He said, "Carter Jameson, 10-13Z, Queensboro Bridge." He explained their predicament.

"What was that code?"

"Civilian clothed officer in trouble," he said. "Put your seat belt on."

She scrambled to click the belt into place.

Carter patted the seat between them. Frosty jumped up. "Help me put the center seat belt on Frosty."

"What's happening?" She stretched the seat belt over Frosty, as he craned his neck behind him, barking into her ear.

The truck roared up right behind them.

"Brace yourself," Carter instructed. "I have a bad feeling about this." Fear infused his tone, betraying the gravity of the situation.

Her body tensed, and she dug her fingers into the seat to brace herself.

With a rev of its big engine, the truck struck the back of their vehicle. The vibration of the hit jolted through Rachelle. Her head bounced off the back seat. Their car fishtailed. Their driver lost control of the wheel, sending the car spinning.

The big truck lurched forward. Rachelle ducked and covered her head as the large silver grill rammed into her side of the vehicle. The sickening sound of metal crunching as the car buckled inward filled the interior. The car slammed into the concrete barrier, keeping them from going over the side of the bridge.

Terrified, Rachelle prayed, "Lord, please, get us out of this."

The trajectory of the town car jerked to a halt. For a moment, Rachelle opened her eyes, then quickly shielded them from the glaring light still shining through the passenger side window.

Carter grabbed at her buckle. "We need to get out."

Before he could unbuckle her, the engine on the big truck rumbled. Fearing her legs would be crushed, Rachelle drew her legs up onto the seat an instant before the side door crumbled inward, bending with a loud shriek. Glass flew through the air and she barely felt the pricks as tiny shards hit her skin.

The big truck pushed their car like it was nothing more than a child's toy.

"Save yourself," Carter yelled to the car driver.

The driver managed to extract himself and stumbled away from the car to safety.

Carter opened the sunroof. "Unhook yourself," he instructed Rachelle. "And Frosty. Hurry!"

He climbed out through the window and reached back inside to help Frosty out onto the roof of the car.

Heart pounding in her ears, she grasped Carter's outstretched hand. He pulled her through just as the truck squished the metal frame of the car.

"This way!" Carter took her hand and drew her onto the top of the concrete barrier. Frosty jumped off what was left of their car onto the road and barked, the frantic sound heartrending.

Beneath her feet, the barrier shook as the car broke through a chunk of cement and the back end dangled over the river.

Surefooted, Carter ran across the barrier to safety. Rachelle's strappy sandals slipped. For a moment, her arms cartwheeled, before she bent her knees and crouched, clinging to the barrier with both hands.

"Move forward," Carter yelled. "You can do it!"

She crawled as best she could until she cleared the front end of the car. Carter reached for her and drew her to his chest as gunfire erupted from the cab of the big truck. Taking her by the hand, he ran with her in a hunched, serpentine fashion toward the line of cars that had stopped.

"Down! Everyone get down," Carter yelled at the people who'd climbed out of their cars.

The pinging of bullets hitting cars and spitting asphalt shuddered through Rachelle. She couldn't believe this. Why were they so determined to kill her?

TWELVE

The sound of sirens punctuated the air. Carter dragged Rachelle down behind the tail end of a large newspaper delivery van. Frosty sat beside them. She buried her face in the dog's fur. The irony wasn't lost on her, and she would have laughed if she weren't so frightened. Here she was, desperately trying to solve Chief Jordan Jameson's murder, following clues that led her to Miles Landau, and she might die hiding behind a newspaper's van.

They heard the squeal of tires on pavement and the roar of the big truck's engine. Carter glanced around the side of the van. "They're leaving."

She gripped his shoulder and peered around him to see the big heavy hauling truck tearing down the roadway away from them, its horn blaring as cars that had stopped on the other side of the accident either scrambled to get out of the way or were pushed out of the way by the heavy grill.

"You're okay," Carter told her.

She nodded, grateful once again for his quick thinking.

For the next hour, there was organized chaos as uniformed officers and other K-9 Unit officers, along with their dogs, converged on the scene. Medics saw to the injured.

Rachelle had sustained a few cuts from broken glass on her shoulders, hands and face. The paramedics also confirmed she hadn't sustained any injuries from her earlier attack. Carter's hand was bandaged for a cut and a shard of glass had to be removed from one of Frosty's paws.

Once the paramedics released her, Rachelle followed Carter to a K-9 Unit vehicle. Her heart beat too fast and her hands shook as she accepted a bottle of water from a tall, brown-haired, brown-eyed officer. Beside him sat a handsome bloodhound, whose deep chocolate eyes studied her with a tilt of his droopy-jowled head.

"Thank you," she said to the officer.

"My pleasure. Name's Reed Branson," Reed told her, his voice low and empathic. "You two have had an exciting evening."

"That's an understatement," Carter muttered

as he tilted a bottle of water to his lips and drank deeply.

"Hop in," Reed said, gesturing to his vehicle. "I've been instructed by the chief to get you both home safely."

"I need to go to the station to interrogate the suspect arrested earlier," Carter told him.

Reed shrugged. "Take it up with your brother." He opened the door. "Until I hear otherwise, get in."

"I should get my own rig, anyway," Carter stated. He held out his hand for Rachelle.

She allowed him to help her into the back seat while Reed put his dog and Frosty into the dog compartment. Carter sat up front on the drive to the house in Rego Park.

When they arrived at the Jamesons', Carter handed her off to his parents, then he and Frosty left in his official vehicle. She burned to go with him, to hear him interrogate the suspect and learn if this man worked for the person responsible for Chief Jordan Jameson's murder.

She would have to wait and see if Carter would divulge any information to her. For now, she just wanted to ease the aches and pain with a hot shower and a good night's sleep. If such a thing was even possible.

* * *

The next three days went by in a blur for Carter. Between dealing with the aftermath of the attempts on Rachelle's life and doing his certification competitions, he was both wired and exhausted.

And unfortunately, no closer to taking down Miles Landau. The thug from The Metropolitan Museum of Art who had attacked Rachelle had lawyered up and wasn't talking. They had him dead to rights on attempted kidnapping and attempted murder. Still, his lawyer maintained that Attilo Hunt was acting alone and had nothing more to say. And unfortunately, the police department couldn't connect Attilo to Miles Landau.

And the haul truck hadn't been found, despite every cop in all five boroughs searching high and low for some sign of the destructive vehicle.

By the morning of the police dog field trials public demonstrations, Carter was wishing he wasn't competing. He was afraid he wouldn't be able to concentrate.

Ellie appeared in the doorway to Carter's bedroom. She'd dressed herself in the unicorn-covered dress Rachelle had apparently purchased for her on their shopping excursion before the fund-raiser ball. The whimsical motif soothed Carter's ragged emotions a little.

"Can I go downstairs for breakfast?"

Needing a few more minutes alone to gather his thoughts, he said, "Sure. I'll be down shortly."

Over the past week he'd tried unsuccessfully to ignore the tension between him and Rachelle that ebbed and flowed in a disturbing way he had never experienced.

When he was away from her, he wondered what she was doing, if she was safe. And every once in a while he'd catch a phantom whiff of lavender and think she was nearby. And then, when he returned home at night, she'd be there with his parents, Katie and Ellie. They'd have dinner ready and would gather like a family. And he'd want to pull Rachelle into his arms and kiss her again.

He didn't know how much more of her being within the bosom of his family he could take without losing his sanity.

But today, he couldn't think about her and his unexpected and unwanted feelings for her. Today he had to focus on the course. Today was about him and Frosty representing the NYC K-9 Command Unit against over forty other teams from all over the nation.

He grabbed his duffel bag filled with all of

Frosty's paraphernalia and water bottles for them both, plus a few granola bars, and headed down to his parents' apartment, determined to keep Rachelle out of his head and his heart.

Rachelle sat at the patio table across from Katie. She opened her flowered notebook and found a blank page. Katie had offered to talk to her about her marriage to Jordan. An unexpected boon. Rachelle picked up her pen, held it poised over the page. "How did you two meet?"

"He taught the self-defense class I took when I first moved to Queens." Katie rubbed her tummy with a sad smile. "I thought he was so handsome, but I didn't talk to him. But then he and Snapper came to Rego Park Elementary School to do a demonstration. And oddly enough he recognized me."

"Why oddly?"

Katie shrugged. "I just never imagined that a man like him would take notice of someone like me."

Rachelle reached across the table to place her hand over Katie's. "I understand the sentiment. But from everything I've learned about Jordan Jameson he was a rare man and I'm sure he was smitten with you from the moment he saw you."

Katie nodded, her gaze unfocused on the yard, where Frosty lay on the grass watching the two puppies tugging on the same toy. "We didn't have a long engagement. In retrospect, I wish we had taken more time to—"

The back screen door banged open and Carter walked out. His gaze zeroed in on Rachelle like a heat-seeking missile. "What are you doing?"

Taken aback by his less than friendly demeanor, she sat up straighter and said, "Good morning to you, too."

He glanced at the little flowered notebook in front of her and the pink pen her hand. "You're interviewing Katie," he accused. "You're still writing an article about Jordan, aren't you?"

She closed her notebook and very slowly set the pen on top. "Yes, I am."

"You promised me you would stop this."

She narrowed her gaze and leaned her elbows on the table. "Carter, I never promised you anything. I told you I would hand over my notes and research. I never said I'd stop writing this article." Uncovering the truth was too important, especially now that she knew and cared for the Jameson family. And adding the personal touches to the story of Jordan's life and love would make him more real to the reader. She wanted people to care about Jordan as a man as well as the chief of the NYC K-9 Command Unit.

"Carter, it's okay," Katie said. "I offered—"

He held up a hand, stopping her. "No, it's not okay, Katie. She's using our family to further her own career."

"Daddy!" Ellie ran out of the house. "Grandma and I finished our puzzle. Isn't it time to go?"

"Yes. It is." Carter's voice sounded a bit strangled.

Ellie skirted around Carter and climbed up on Rachelle's lap. "You're coming with us, right?"

Loving the feel of the little girl in her arms, Rachelle held Carter's gaze. She wouldn't go where she wasn't wanted, but she wasn't going to make it easy for him. Not when she longed to be a part of the Jameson clan for as long as possible. "If it's still okay with your father."

For a long moment, he didn't respond. Rachelle wavered in her determination to stand her ground. She should bow out because he apparently didn't want her to go.

"If Rachelle wants to attend, she's free to," he finally said. He directed his focus on Ellie. "Can I have a blessing kiss?"

Ellie slipped off Rachelle's lap and hurried to her father. She took his face in her little hands and kissed his forehead, his nose, each cheek and his chin. "May you be blessed with a good run today. Whether you win or lose, Daddy, I will love you no matter what."

The tender show of love between daughter and father had Rachelle's eyes tearing up.

Carter placed a kiss on Ellie's golden head, then he whistled for Frosty. The dog trotted toward the porch stairs with the puppies scampering close behind. Frosty followed Carter into the house, the screen door closing behind them. A moment later, Ivy stepped out with treats for the puppies, which she gave to Ellie. The little girl and the puppies raced around the yard.

"Carter's not used to sharing Ellie with somebody outside the family," Ivy said without preamble. "Ellie's become quite attached to you."

"And I her," Rachelle said. "I'm sure Carter wants to protect her. At some point I will be leaving." The thought brought a pang of loss she wasn't looking forward to.

Ivy sat next to Katie. "That could be true."

Could be true? What did she mean by that?

Rachelle wanted to probe Ivy's words but before she could ask, Ivy continued, "You should have seen Carter in the early days. He needed our help, but boy, he wanted to do it all himself. But he's like that." Ivy sat next to Katie. "The doer has a hard time delegating. Unlike Noah, who is a master delegator. He would delegate doing the dishes when he was a kid." Ivy chuckled. "I would come into the kitchen and the three boys would be washing and drying and loading the dishwasher. And there would be Noah, supervising."

Rachelle itched to write these details down but refrained as Carter's words about using his family echoed in her head. "Who's older? Noah or Carter?"

"Noah, by a couple of years." Ivy shook her head. "Those two were always vying for attention."

"I'd guess Jordan was the one loading the dishwasher," Katie said. "He liked things done a certain way."

"Yes," Ivy said. "Jordy would come in and re-arrange the dishwasher behind me sometimes." Her smile faded. "I really miss him."

Katie reached over to awkwardly hug Ivy. "We all miss him."

Rachelle dropped her gaze, feeling out of place.

Ellie ran up the porch stairs. "Are we gonna go?"

Ivy wiped at her eyes. "Yes, we are. Grandpa made some sandwiches so we don't have to buy anything at the concession stand."

"Oh," Ellie grumbled. "I wanted to get some cotton candy."

"That's between you and your daddy." Ivy headed back inside. "You know how he feels about sugar."

Rachelle took Ellie's hand. "They have cotton candy? I haven't had cotton candy since I was your age." She winked at the child. "I may just have to buy myself some."

Ellie grinned at her. "You'll share, right?"

"Of course."

Katie rose from the patio chair and looked at Rachelle. "You're playing with fire."

Rachelle shrugged. "What's a little more disapproval in my life?"

The stadium seats were filled. The crowd buzzed as Rachelle filed through the entrance of the sports complex housing the police dog field trials. The large grass field was dotted with various pieces of equipment like those in the NYC K-9 Command Unit's training center.

Rachelle hadn't been sure what to expect and was bemused by the excitement in the air and the multitude of people who'd come out to watch the K-9 dogs and their handlers demonstrate their abilities.

Her look must've given her away, because Alex said, "Folks from all over the region come out for these trials. It's a big deal."

"So I'm gathering." She followed the Jamesons to their seats, which were in a really good place where they could see the whole field. Zach and his wife, Violet, along with Mr. and Mrs.

Griffin were already seated. A sense of belonging seeped through her and it tore her up inside to know there would be a day when she'd have to leave them.

She sat between Ellie and Alex. "How often do they hold these trials?"

"The regional ones are twice yearly," Alex explained.

"I'm very blessed that I was here for this one." Rachelle traced Carter's name on the glossy program. There was another team from the NYC K-9 Command Unit listed: Officer Luke Hathaway and his German shepherd, Bruno.

Katie said, "We'll be blessed if we don't walk out of here with our backsides numb."

Rachelle had to laugh. The seats weren't the best, but they weren't the worst she'd ever sat on.

"Hi, everyone." A pretty woman with long brown hair and big blue eyes scooted into their row and sat on the other side of Katie.

Katie hugged the woman. "Sophie, I wasn't sure you'd make it."

"I wouldn't miss Luke and Bruno for anything," Sophie said. She leaned forward. "Hi, Ellie."

Ellie jumped up and shimmied past Rachelle to give the newcomer a hug.

"Sophie, this is Rachelle Clark," Katie said.

"Rachelle, this is Sophie Walters, Noah's assistant and soon to be Luke Hathaway's bride."

"We talked on the phone when you called to ask about interviewing Noah," Sophie said, extending her hand that bore a beautiful engagement ring.

"Yes, we did. Thank you for your help that day. I was happy Noah offered up his brother," Rachelle said as she shook Sophie's hand. If Noah hadn't suggested she talk to Carter, she wouldn't be here right now. Literally. Carter had saved her life that day and many times since.

As the announcer welcomed the attendees and introduced the participants, Rachelle settled in her seat with Ellie on her lap. A roar went up from the crowd as each duo was presented. Rachelle yelled and clapped along with the Jamesons when Carter and Frosty trotted onto the field. They also cheered for Luke Hathaway and Bruno.

The demonstration got underway. Rachelle followed along with the program as the teams competed on the different obstacles. Her heart raced every time it was Carter and Frosty's turn to compete. The pair was so in sync. She was sure they'd win.

"Okay," Alex said, in a lull between events. "If anybody wants anything from the concession stand you better go do it now. In about ten minutes there's an official break."

Katie pulled herself to her feet. "I need to find the restroom."

Ellie tugged on Rachelle's sleeve. "Cotton candy?" she whispered.

With a grin, Rachelle stood. "We'll go with you."

They shimmied their way out of the stands to the main concession area. Katie waddled away in search of a restroom, while Rachelle and Ellie joined the line at the concession stand.

As they moved forward, Rachelle could feel a presence behind her. Not liking the invasion of her personal bubble, Rachelle glanced over her shoulder and locked gazes with a young woman with black hair beneath a baseball cap. Rachelle moved forward and the woman did, as well. Chalking it up to the New York way, she ignored how much the woman was crowding her space.

There were only three more people ahead of them when the woman latched on to Rachelle's shoulder. She leaned in close. "If you don't want anything to happen to this pretty little girl and her father," the woman whispered in a raspy tone into Rachelle's ear, "you better stop snooping into things that are none of your business."

Rachelle whipped around, shrugging off the

woman's hand. The woman darted out of the line and blended into the crowd. Heart racing with the ominous words ringing inside her head, Rachelle fought back hot tears of frustration. It was one thing to put her life, and even Carter's, in danger. But to put Ellie in jeopardy was unacceptable.

Rachelle could not allow anything to happen to Carter's sweet little girl.

It was time for Rachelle to leave the safety of the Jameson home, as soon as possible.

THIRTEEN

Carter had just tucked Ellie into bed and kissed her good-night when he heard a knock on the front door to the apartment. Since Noah was still working, Carter quietly shut Ellie's bedroom door and hurried to open the apartment door to find his mother standing there. Unexpected disappointment shoved him hard in the chest. He wasn't sure why he had been hoping Rachelle would be at the door. They'd hardly spoken two words to each other all evening.

"You better get downstairs," his mother said by way of greeting. "Rachelle's packing and planning to leave."

The news was like a punch to the gut. "What do you mean she's leaving?"

"I don't know. Something must've happened at the field trials because she's been…" His mom paused, seeming to search for the right word.

"Subdued?"

"Yes. Exactly."

He'd noticed after the competition that she'd been very un-Rachelle-like. She'd been quiet and reserved when they all went to Griffin's Diner for a celebratory meal. Though he and Frosty placed second and Luke and Bruno placed third behind the team from Boston PD, Carter had been jazzed to represent the NYC K-9 Command Unit and was grateful for placing so high.

"Go," his mother urged. "I'll stay with Ellie."

He hurried downstairs, belatedly realizing he had no shoes. Didn't matter. He needed to find out what was going on with Rachelle. He entered his parents' apartment, and his father, standing sentinel, pointed down the hallway. With a nod, Carter strode to Rachelle's closed bedroom door and knocked.

"Come in," she said.

He pushed the door open and saw the suitcase she was packing on the bed was already nearly full.

She glanced up at him. A little V appeared between her eyebrows. "What are you doing here?" Her eyes widened with fear. "Is Ellie okay?"

The quiver in her voice sent an alarm through his system. "Of course she's okay. Why wouldn't she be?"

She let out a noisy breath and turned back to her task of packing. "Good."

He put his hand over hers, stilling her movements. "Rachelle, tell me what's going on."

She kept her head bent, her eyes downcast. Light from the overheard fixture created shadows over her cheeks. "Why does something have to be going on?"

"You're packing your bags. Why are you going?"

"You can't make me stay here."

He drew her hands to his chest, forcing her to face him even though she refused to meet his gaze. "You're right, I can't make you stay," he said carefully. "But I don't understand why you want to leave now. Is it because I was upset with you earlier?"

A pained expression flittered across her face. "No. That has nothing to do with this."

"Then what has happened? Tell me."

She tugged her hands away and moved several steps back. "Nothing. Nothing happened."

"Right. You haven't been acting yourself ever since the field trials. My mom even noticed."

Rachelle bit her lip. She seemed to be wrestling with a decision she was struggling to make.

"Talk to me," he pressed. "Trust me."

Finally, she said, "It's not safe here. I need to leave."

Her words made zero sense to Carter. "Of course it's safe here. You're safer here than anywhere else."

She shook her head. "You don't understand. They know."

His breath stalled in his lungs. A chill of dread worked down his spine. "They who?"

"Whoever's targeting me. Miles, if he's the killer. And if he's not, then *whoever is* Jordan's killer. Maybe more than one person is responsible. I don't know, but somebody knows I'm here and—" She clamped her lips together.

"And what?" He stalked forward, stopping within an inch of her. He gripped her shoulders. "Tell me what happened."

She swallowed, looking trapped and afraid. He eased his hold on her to cup her cheek. "Rachelle, whatever it is, whatever happened to you, whoever threatened you, you can tell me. I will keep you safe."

Turning her head into his palm, she closed her eyes. When she opened them, they were filled with determination and she stepped out of his grasp. "It's not me I'm afraid for. It's Ellie."

His heart dropped. "What do you mean?"

"Today when Ellie and I went to the concession stand, a woman told me that I better back off or they would hurt you and Ellie." She shook her head. "I can't let anything happen to your little girl."

A deep fury ignited in his chest. Not directed at Rachelle, but at these unnamed, faceless people who were threatening her and now his daughter. "You don't have to worry. You're both safe here. I will get armed guards to cover the front of the house and the back."

Darting around him, she resumed packing. "I'm leaving. You can't stop me. If I'm gone then she's out of danger."

"But you won't be out of danger." The thought of something happening to her tore him up inside. He couldn't let her leave.

"It doesn't matter," she insisted. "What matters is Ellie."

He frowned at her logic. "You do matter."

She waved away his protest. "Ellie is all that matters. Her safety. Your parents' safety. Your safety." Her voice broke on her last words. "I've brought nothing but trouble into your life."

Now she was being silly. "Rachelle, listen to reason."

She held up a hand. "Carter, I am not under arrest. You can't force me to stay here."

From outside the house a horn blared.

"That's my ride." She zipped up the suitcase and pulled it off the bed. She grabbed her purse and slung it over her shoulder. "Please, just let me go."

"Where are you going?" His heart beat so fast he thought it might jump out of his chest. He wanted to demand she stay put but she was right, he couldn't stop her. She was an adult with the right to exercise the free will God gave everyone. But he wished he could compel her somehow to stay within the protection of his family, within his protection.

She dragged her suitcase across the carpeted floor toward the door. He rushed forward. "Here, let me take that."

He considered holding her suitcase hostage. Instead, he helped her out to the curb, where a black town car sat waiting.

The driver jumped out and came around to take the suitcase and stashed it in the trunk.

Carter wanted make sure the guy was legit. "Let me see your license and registration."

The driver paused with confusion on his face. "Excuse me?"

He heard Rachelle give a little sigh. He didn't care. She was going to be safe no matter what it took.

"Carter." She put a hand on his arm and allowed the driver to slip back into his seat.

He faced Rachelle. A desperate sensation

curled through him. She let go of him to put her hand on the rear passenger door handle.

He stopped the door from closing. "Rachelle, this is crazy. Tell me you aren't going back to your apartment."

She gave him a droll look. "Of course not."

"Are you going home to Georgia?"

Letting out a beleaguered sigh, she shook her head. "No. I'll be at The Elms. It has a twenty-four-hour concierge, state-of-the-art security and I have a room high up."

"I should go with you," he said.

"You have no shoes on."

"Give me five minutes to put some on."

She tugged on the door. "Carter, just please let go."

He didn't want to let go. Deep inside he never wanted to let her go. And the realization nearly took him to his knees.

"Call me when you get there," he insisted. "And check in frequently."

"I will. Thank you for all you've done. Keep Ellie safe."

"Of course." His stomach clenched. He wanted to reach out and cup her cheek, to smooth away the worry from her brow. His kept his hands at his sides. "Be careful."

"Of course." She gave him the smile she used on him when she was convincing him she knew what she was doing, or her boss when trying to get the assignment she wanted. Carter realized the truth behind her smile: false bravado. Was she trying to convince the world, or herself?

Yet here she was, making the brave choices anyway.

And he had no option but to let her. He couldn't compel her to stay. He had no say in her life. Short of begging...

"Please reconsider. We can put you in a safe house somewhere else. I can't protect you if you run away."

"I'm not running away. Don't you understand?" Her voice rose. "I couldn't live with myself if something happened to your family because of me. If you can arrange a safe house then I'll go there but until then—" Her lips firmed and steel entered her eyes. She tugged on the door again.

He released the handle and she shut the door. The car rolled away, disappearing around the corner.

Would he see her again?

And his heart ached with the knowledge that he was well on his way to unwittingly falling for Rachelle.

Guilt swamped Carter and he lifted his eyes heavenward. "Lord, I don't understand. How can I allow her into my heart?"

He never understood how it could still beat inside his chest since the day Helen died. He'd been living for Ellie and Ellie alone. Now there was somebody else he wanted in his life. But he couldn't do it. He couldn't dishonor the woman who had given birth to his daughter.

He turned to head back into the house and found his father standing on the porch. "You let her go."

The accusation was like a slap. "I had no choice. I couldn't hold her hostage."

"Do you know where she's going?" Alex asked.

"Yes. The Elms."

"On the Upper East Side? I know the place. It's in a good neighborhood."

"But she's alone and unprotected. I have to arrange for a safe house." He swiped a hand through his hair in frustration. "I'll call the hotel security and make sure they are aware she's in danger."

"Both are good ideas," his dad said. "But more importantly, did you tell her how you feel?"

"How I feel?" Carter moved past his father toward the staircase. "I don't know what you mean."

Alex grabbed him by the arm, stopping him in his tracks. "Don't try to deny it. I know you too well. You love that young lady. But you're just too bullheaded to face the truth."

"I am not in love with Rachelle. I can't do that to Ellie. I can't betray Helen." He needed to build up the walls around his heart once again. To protect himself from pain.

Alex put his hand on Carter's shoulder and turned him so they were face-to-face. The porch light shone on his dad's face, revealing the compassion in his expression. "Son, Helen would want you to be happy. She would want Ellie to be happy. Rachelle makes you both happy."

Carter shook his head in a futile attempt to protest what his heart already knew. Ellie loved Rachelle, and he could if he allowed himself to. "But there's no future for me with Rachelle. There just can't be. I'm not ready to let her or anyone else in, Dad. What if something happens to her?" His voice cracked, and he jerked out of his father's grasp. He ran for the staircase leading to his apartment as if he could outrun the truth of his fears.

"Love is worth the risk," he heard his father say. "Excuses will only leave you lonely."

The next day Carter's stomach hurt, and acrid worry chomped through him as he sat at his desk. Rachelle had called when she'd reached the hotel and had given him her room number as promised. He expected her to check in this morning but so far hadn't heard from her, which caused his blood pressure to rise with every passing second.

Last night, he'd talked to the hotel security and they seemed competent. Still, he didn't like the idea of her alone and vulnerable even for a short time.

He'd spent the past hour arranging for a safe house, which was taking longer than he'd expected, much to his frustration. Jumping through red tape was like eating shards of glass. Nothing was within his control and he hated that he couldn't speed up the process.

From his office doorway, Noah called out, "Miles Landau has been spotted. Everyone is gathered in the conference room."

Carter's heart rate tripled. Finally, if they could get Landau, Rachelle would be out of danger.

Carter rushed to the conference room and squeezed in between Tony and Reed.

"We've had Miles Landau under surveillance," Noah said to the group. "Today he was seen entering the warehouse in Flushing. I just now received word that a detective from the Brooklyn precinct leaned on one of his confidential informants and discovered a way into Landau's crew. The CI's cousin or something.

He says Miles has been ranting and raving about a reporter."

Carter's heart froze for a moment, then pounded in big painful beats. The property he'd purchased after he'd served his sentence from the first time Jordan had sent him to prison. Clearly he'd resumed his illegal activities, but he has mostly been obsessing over some reporter…

"He has to be talking about Rachelle." She obviously hadn't given up on doing her own investigating into Miles while at the Elms. "We have to pick him up before he finds her."

"We will," Noah told him. "Unfortunately, he sent thugs out to take care of the problem."

Carter slammed his hand on the conference room table. "How do they know how to find her?"

"I have no idea," Noah told him. "We'll bring the whole weight of the NYPD down on his head. But first we have to get to Rachelle before he and his minions do. I've sent local officers to her location."

Carter was already heading out the door. "I'm heading there now."

Rachelle sat at the desk in front of the window of her twenty-fourth-floor hotel room. She was safe so high up, and the view of the city in the distance was spectacular. There was a watchful doorman and video security cameras everywhere.

Though she missed the Jamesons something fierce, she'd made the right decision. Now there was no chance Ellie could be hurt because of Rachelle.

This time in isolation had given Rachelle an opportunity to finish and turn in the two articles she'd been working on. Her boss had been very pleased with the story she'd done on the celebrity ball fund-raiser for autism. And for her article about the police dog field trials, she couldn't help but highlight Carter and Frosty a bit more than she did any of the other dog and officer teams. They were local heroes and she wanted to make sure everyone knew it.

With both of the stories in the can, she turned her mind back to Miles Landau. She looked at the information on her laptop computer screen. She had found more information on Miles's company. MiLand, Inc. held stock in a trucking company. One that supplied heavy hauling trucks like the one that had tried to crush them on the Queensboro bridge.

Tapping her fingers on the desktop, Rachelle wondered aloud, "What are you up to, Miles Landau? What do a warehouse in Flushing, a boat and a trucking company have to do with Chief Jordan Jameson's murder?"

The hotel's desk phone rang and she froze. No one would call her through the hotel's system. She checked her cell phone on the charger. Three missed calls from Carter. She'd left the ringer off.

She snatched up the receiver and said, "Hello?"

"Why aren't you answering your cell phone?" Carter's terse words were accompanied by the sound of a siren.

"Sorry. The battery died this morning. And I forgot to turn the ringer back on. I turn it off at night when I go to bed." Dread gripped her in a tight vise. "Did something happen? Ellie?"

"Ellie's fine. However, Miles Landau knows where you are. We have to get you to safety. I'm on my way to you now. Almost there. But local officers will be arriving shortly."

Her stomach dropped with trepidation. She stood and paced. "How did he find me?"

"I don't know. What have you been doing that would draw his attention?"

A pang of dismay made her wince. "I've been searching through more public records." She removed the thumb drive she'd used to back up her work from the laptop and shut the device down. "He owns stock in a trucking company that serves the whole Eastern Seaboard."

"You know how dangerous he is. Why do you insist on pursuing your own investigation?"

She could feel the reprimand through the phone line. "You can't tell a zebra to change its stripes," she told him. "I'm a reporter and I am going to find out why Miles Landau wants me dead and how he's connected to your brother's murder."

She thought about the phone call she'd made earlier. Better to come clean and face his wrath over the phone rather than in person. "So I—uh—called the trucking company Miles has stock in posing as a potential client. I asked the woman who answered about their fees, potential routes and drivers." She looked around the room for a place to hide the thumb drive.

"Is that all?" The exasperation in his tone reached through the line and tweaked her conscience.

Pulse thumping in her veins, she grimaced as she attempted to drag the desk chair beneath the air vent in the ceiling. The phone wouldn't reach. She paused to say, "I asked if I could speak to Miles Landau."

He groaned. "They could have called the number back and found out where you were staying."

"I realize that now," she said. "Hold on." She put the receiver on the desk so she could put the chair under the air vent, then stepped up and slid the small, silver memory stick through the slats. She jumped off the chair and picked up the receiver.

"Rachelle!"

Carter's frantic yelling pierced her ear. "Here. Sorry, sorry. I was hiding the backup of my computer."

"There's a street fair blocking off the road," he told her. In the background she heard music and voices. "We're on foot. Just minutes away. Haven't the local officers arrived?"

"They haven't," she said, the edges of panic closing in on her. "I'll put my shoes on and meet you downstairs."

"No! Stay put. Wait for me."

The sound of the hotel room doorknob rattling raised the fine hairs on her arms. Panic squeezed her chest. She could barely breathe. "Carter, someone's at the door."

FOURTEEN

"Don't take any chances—hide!"

Taking Carter's order to hide seriously, Rach-elle dropped the receiver and ran toward the bathroom in hopes to lock herself inside long enough for Carter to reach her. She'd taken two steps when a loud thwack reverberated through the room and the door splintered, the locks pop-ping open. Two men entered with guns drawn.

For a split second, she froze in shock. Then self-preservation kicked in and she darted for the bathroom.

Thug One vaulted forward and caught her with big, rough hands. "Oh no, you don't."

Thug Two grabbed her laptop from the desk. "Let's go."

Hoping to buy enough time for Carter to reach her, she resisted, kicking and screaming.

"You're a little wildcat." Thug One shoved her forward. She dropped to her hands and knees. If he wanted to take her, he was going to have to carry her. Instead, he raised his gun, aiming for her head.

"No!" Thug Two shouted. "The boss wants to take care of her himself."

Thug One growled and reached out to yank her to her feet. He towered over her as he cursed at her and dragged her toward the door.

In an effort to continue to stall them, she said, "I need my shoes."

A feral grin spread over Thug One's face. "You don't need shoes where you're going."

If he'd meant to ratchet up her fear, he'd succeeded.

With his gun pressed into her rib cage, Thug One forced her out of the room and down the hall to the elevator. Her bare toes sank deeply into the surprisingly plush hall carpet she hadn't even noticed before now. She prayed the doors would open and Carter and Frosty would be there. Her heart plummeted when the car arrived empty. Thug One shoved her inside.

"Why?" she asked as the elevator descended. Neither man answered.

"Miles Landau is your boss, right?" she pressed.

"Shut up," Thug Two said.

"Did he or you kill Chief Jordan Jameson?"

The two men exchanged a confused look before Thug Two repeated, "Shut up."

They reached the lobby and stepped out.

Rachelle's gaze sought Robert, the concierge, but he wasn't at his post. Dread seized her and tightened her chest. "What did you do to Robert?" And where was the security team? The police officers?

Without getting an answer, Rachelle was shoved out the sliding doors of the hotel. Frantic, she searched the crowd. Half a block away she spied Carter and Frosty pushing their way through the crowded street as they raced toward her.

The squeal of tires jerked her attention to a black sedan as it halted at the corner.

Thug One jammed the gun hard into her ribs. "This way."

Panicking, she twisted around, her gaze locking with Carter's. "Carter!"

"Halt! Police!" came his cry.

He released Frosty, and the dog raced forward. Thug One raised his gun. Fearing for Frosty, Rachelle rammed her elbow into his side. He let out a grunt, then wrapped his arm around her body, using her as a shield as he hauled her backward toward the sedan that had pulled up, driven by a third man. Thug Two opened the back door and tossed her computer inside. "Move it! Let's go."

Frosty barked and lunged. Thug One jerked Rachelle around like a rag doll, keeping her in front of him. They reached the sedan and the thug climbed in, dragging her with him. Frosty instead latched on to the arm of the other bad guy, snarling viciously and tugging him away from the car as the engine revved and the sedan shot forward, taking her away from Carter, Frosty and any hope of rescue.

Chest heaving with panic and adrenaline, Carter aimed his drawn weapon at the man trying to shake Frosty off his arm.

"Out!" Carter commanded Frosty. The dog released his hold on the assailant and backed up, his tail high and his teeth bared.

"Don't move," he yelled at the man.

Carter watched helplessly as the sedan carrying Rachelle away roared down the street with its horn blaring, forcing pedestrians and other cars to get out of the way. The vehicle careened around the corner and disappeared.

With one hand still holding his gun, Carter used his radio to call in the license plate of the sedan that had just kidnapped Rachelle. The dog whined.

"I know, buddy." They'd failed to protect Rachelle, and he could only imagine the horror of what would happen to her now.

Carter quickly handcuffed Rachelle's attacker. "Where are they taking her?"

The man smirked. "Lawyer."

"Tell me." Carter shook the man.

Frosty growled a warning.

Gaze darting between Carter and Frosty, the man replied, "I said lawyer."

Several police cruisers screeched to a halt in front of The Elms. Carter had no choice but to pass the guy off to another member of the NYPD, who read him his rights before putting him in the back of a cruiser just as Noah arrived along with several other members of the NYC K-9 Command Unit.

Carter told Noah about the sedan that had taken Rachelle away.

"We have to find her," he told his brother.

Noah clamped a hand on his shoulder. "We will, Carter. I'll put out a BOLO."

"The warehouse," Carter said. "He'll take her there."

"We've got the place locked up tight," Noah told him. "Miles wasn't there. Apparently he no longer deals drugs but weapons. We rounded up his men and they all lawyered up."

Just like the other two criminals working for Miles.

"Where are the local officers who were supposed to be here?" Noah asked.

Dread squeezed Carter's chest. "I didn't see them or the hotel security."

Noah's jaw firmed. "We'll search the building for them. And pray they are alive."

Frustration beat a steady pulse through Carter's veins. "Rachelle said something about a trucking company that Miles's company owns stock in."

"That's something," Noah said. "Did she give you the name and location?"

"No. But it would be on her computer in her hotel room."

He whirled and raced into the hotel with Frosty at his heels.

At the elevator, Carter jammed his finger on the call button as he heard Noah saying to the others, "Find the doorman, the security guards and the local officers who were sent to this location. Check the hotel's video and get it to Danielle so we can identify Miss Clark's kidnappers."

The elevator arrived, the door sliding open. Carter and Frosty entered. Before the doors could close, Reed and his dog, Jessie, stepped inside.

"I can't let you go through this alone, man," Reed said.

Appreciating his friend's support, Carter nodded, not sure he could speak without his voice revealing the fear tearing him up inside. What if he didn't reach Rachelle in time? What if he lost her, too?

He couldn't take another death of someone he… He couldn't finish the thought.

On the twenty-fourth floor he stepped out of the elevator and ran down the hall to Rachelle's room. The door hung off its hinges. His heart lurched. He remembered the horrifying sound of the door busting open and Rachelle's screams. He shuddered as nausea roiled through him.

Letting his emotions get the better of him wouldn't help Rachelle. Determined to keep focused on doing the job, he entered the room with Frosty. The dog sniffed the carpet. Behind him, Reed and Jessie entered.

Rachelle's laptop wasn't on the desk by the window. He opened the closet and the drawers of the dresser. "Her computer isn't here." He snapped his fingers. "The thumb drive. She hid one somewhere in here."

The desk chair had been pulled to the center of the room. Her cell phone was on the charger, plugged in to the outlet on the desk. The hotel phone lay on the floor.

While Reed searched under the bed and between the mattress and box spring, Carter circled the chair. Why was this here? He tilted his head back and eyed the vent in the ceiling. Would she have hidden the device there?

He stepped onto the chair and probed at the vent. She could have shoved the USB between the slats. He dug into his duty belt for his multitool. He used the screwdriver portion of the versatile tool to undo the screws holding the vent plate in place. When he removed the plate, a small, silver memory stick fell to the floor. Frosty sniffed at it and whined, no doubt picking up Rachelle's scent from the device.

Picking up the thumb drive, Carter said, "We have to get this to Danielle."

Rachelle wasn't surprised when the sedan pulled into the gravel driveway of Smith's Trucking Company in Flushing. The same company that Miles Landau owned stock in. She sent up a prayer that Carter would make Thug Two tell them where to find her. She only wished she'd told Carter where she'd hidden her thumb drive in case Thug Two refused to talk.

Sitting in the back seat next to Thug One, who kept his gun pressed into her side, she looked for possible escape routes as a metal gate closed behind the car. They had passed through an industrial area until they reached the compound, which had a high chain-link fence covered over with sheets of corrugated metal preventing anyone from seeing inside. A dozen large hauling trucks were parked in two rows of six. A building near the front looked like the company office.

If Rachelle managed to get away from her captors she could hide in the trucks or go to the office for help. But would she find help there? Most likely Thug One would only catch her or shoot her as she ran or tried to climb the fence. And she doubted there was anyone on the other side to hear her screams. They were pretty isolated at this far end of the borough.

"It's not too late." She sat forward to address the driver, who'd yet to say a word. "You could let me go. The police know about this place. They'll be here any minute and y'all will go to jail."

Thug One yanked her back as the car rolled to a halt. His wide-set eyes held anger in their depths. "When we're done with you, there won't be anything left for the police to find. Now shut up."

A shiver of terror coursed over her skin at his ominous words. She was hauled unceremoniously out of the sedan. Rocks dug into her bare feet as she was pushed toward a metal building at the back of the property. Biting back yelps of pain, she lurched through the door behind the thug who'd driven them here. The smooth, concrete floor eased the pain in her feet as Thug One continued to poke at her with his gun. She wished Frosty had taken another bite out of the man.

The door clanked closed behind them. Musty and humid, the heat of the day would have been suffocating if not for the large fan whirling overhead, the noise bouncing off the walls. Sunlight filtered through the grimy windows, illuminating the large space. Large crates, stacked two and three high, lined the opposite wall. In the center of the building sat a man at a metal desk. She recognized Miles Landau from the pictures in his police file.

Sweat beaded his bald head. He steepled his hands and stared at her, his dark eyes unnerving. "So you're the pain in my neck. I wanted to see you for myself. You're just a slip of a thing yet so hard to get rid of. Do you have any idea of the trouble you've caused me?"

Thug One shoved her forward. She stumbled a few steps. "Trouble?"

"Yes. My buyers have become nervous from all your snooping." He gestured to the crates. "Now I'm stuck with product I can't move. All because you've been poking around into my life."

"You're back to selling drugs," she said.

Miles barked out a laugh. "I've moved up in

the world." He waved a hand toward the crates. "Show her."

"Boss, I think that's not a good idea," Thug One said.

Miles glared at him. "I don't pay you to think."

The driver of the sedan moved to one of the crates and slid the lid off to reveal multiple weapons inside.

"You've become an illegal arms dealer." That wasn't what had led her to investigate him. "Did you kill Chief Jordan Jameson?"

He narrowed his gaze. "I heard about his death. I can't say I'm too sad as he's the reason I went to prison, but—" he shrugged "—I also would thank him since that's where I made the contacts to start my new business."

Unsure that she believed his protest, she clarified, "Are you saying you didn't kill him?"

"Not me," Miles said. "Is that why you've been snooping into my life? You thought I offed Jameson?"

"You were released only a few days before his death," she said. "You vowed revenge at your trial."

"True. And unfortunate timing, but I didn't kill him." He rose. "However, I won't be able to say the same of you."

Another wave of fear crashed through her. "The police know about this place."

"She's been claiming that all the way here." The driver finally spoke.

"We should just do away with her now," Thug One insisted. "I'll gladly do the deed on behalf of Attilo."

Rachelle thought about the man who now sat in jail after failing to take her at the fund-raising event.

"We can't take the chance that she told the police about this place, too," Miles said. "We have to move. We've already lost the warehouse and the inventory there." He shook his head. "All my hard work destroyed." His lip curled. "I was going to take my time killing you, but now we're in a hurry. Ken, take her out back and don't leave anything for the vultures to take away."

"Gladly." Thug One, Ken, bared his teeth at her like a rabid dog.

She shrank back. "Please, Miles. Don't make things worse for yourself. Killing me isn't going to solve anything."

"Maybe not," Miles said. "But it will send a message to anyone else who tries to mess with me and my operation." He made a rolling gesture with his finger. "Get moving."

Danielle had no trouble accessing the thumb drive's information. Carter grabbed the address of the trucking company and hustled out of headquarters with Reed and Jessie to very end of Flushing where Smith's Trucking was located. They pulled to a stop outside the ten-foot-high chain-link fence lined with sheet metal. Stacking behind them were Noah with Luke Hathaway and Tony Knight along with Carter's youngest brother, Zach.

They gathered at Noah's vehicle. "We'll need bolt cutters," he said, eyeing the fence. "That metal looks thin. Easy to bend."

"Sure hope it's not electric," Luke said.

Carter grabbed a handful of dirt and threw it at the fence. No sparks ignited. "Nope."

"I've got a set in my rig." Tony peeled away.

"Me, too," said Reed.

"Good. I do, too," Noah said. "Zach, you go with Tony and take the west side of the compound. Luke and I will take the east." Noah looked at Carter. "You and Reed head to the back."

"What if they come out the front?" Zach asked.

Noah pointed to the NYPD cruisers pulling up. "Those guys will be waiting to take whoever comes out into custody. They have a stake in arresting Miles, too. The officers that had been dispatched to Rachelle's hotel, along with the hotel security, were found unconscious and tied up in the janitor's closet. One of the officers has a concussion."

Carter was relieved to hear the men were alive.

After retrieving their dogs, the K-9 Unit dispersed.

Carter lifted a prayer they weren't too late to save Rachelle as he and Frosty took off with Reed and Jessie close behind. He kept an eye out for video surveillance equipment but didn't see any.

They reached the back of the compound. Reed cut through the chain-link fence and bent back the sheet of metal and they found themselves facing the backside of a metal outbuilding. They squeezed through, keeping the dogs close.

A low growl emanated from Frosty. Carter gave him the hand signal for silence.

Carter peered around the building, his heart stuttering to a stop at the sight of Rachelle being manhandled by a large, beefy guy—the same guy who'd abducted her from the hotel. He was attempting to drag her toward the fence, but she wasn't making it easy.

Relief that she was still alive and fighting lifted Carter's spirits.

Drawing his weapon, Carter whispered to Reed, "Cover me."

Reed nodded and withdrew his weapon.

Keeping a tight hold on Frosty, Carter stepped out from around the back of the building. "Let her go."

The assailant stilled with one arm wrapped around Rachelle's waist. With his other hand, he reached behind him and produced a gun, which he shoved into her rib cage. "Don't come any closer," he yelled. "I'm taking her with me." He pulled her toward the closest haul truck.

"There's nowhere for you to go," Carter told him. Frosty strained at his lead. "You have nowhere to run."

The door of the metal building banged open and a man came out holding an AK-47 semi-automatic rifle.

"Halt," Reed called as he aimed his weapon at the newcomer.

Without warning, the man holding Rachelle aimed and fired at Carter. The retort of the gun echoed through Carter's head as white-hot pain tore through his leg.

"No!"

Rachelle's cry sliced through Carter's heart. He buckled, going down hard to the ground, losing his hold on Frosty. "Go," he said.

The dog rushed forward.

From all around there were shouts as the K-9 team and officers of the NYPD flooded the compound, quickly subduing the man and leading Miles Landau out of the metal building.

And yet Rachelle's captor refused to give up. He held the gun to her head and backed away. Frosty followed, barking and lunging, but the man was too adept at using Rachelle as a shield.

"Drop your weapon," Noah shouted.

"No way. I'm a dead man if I do," the guy shouted. "She's my ticket out of here."

Carter fought through the agony burning his leg. Using what remained of his energy, Carter lifted his weapon. He met Rachelle's terrified gaze. He prayed she'd understand as he yelled, "Drop!"

Trained to follow the command, Frosty dropped to his belly. A fraction of a second later, Rachelle went limp in the man's arms, creating an opening.

Fearing for Rachelle and knowing in his heart of hearts that he couldn't fail her now, Carter made a difficult choice and fired, striking the man square in the chest. The man crumpled to the ground and Rachelle was free.

Drained, Carter flopped onto his back and stared at the blue sky overhead.

Then Rachelle and Frosty were at his side. Her lavender scent filled his head. Her soft hands soothed his fevered brow. She gathered him in her arms. Frosty whined and licked Carter's cheek. He wanted to reassure them both he was all right. It would take more than a bullet to the leg to do him in. Yet, he couldn't form words. His tongue felt thick. His brain fogged like a window in winter. A chill passed over him. Fire licked at the wound in his leg.

From a distance, he heard Rachelle's sweetly accented voice calling to him. "Stay with me. Please, Carter. Don't you dare leave me."

I won't. The thought flittered through him. *Lie or truth?*

He didn't know. He couldn't hold on to the light. Darkness pulled, the allure of oblivion, where there'd be no more pain. No more heartache.

But Ellie! Rachelle!

They needed him. He fought to stay in the light, to stay with her, but the last of his strength ebbed into the gravel beneath him.

Darkness settled in, scrubbing the edges off the pain as he lost sight of Rachelle's tearstained face.

FIFTEEN

"Help him!" Rachelle held Carter half on her lap. His head lolled to the side, his eyes closed. There was so much blood on the ground, seeping into the earth from the bullet wound just above his knee. She pressed her hands against his leg, but crimson liquid oozed through her fingers. Her heart stalled out. They were going to lose him.

An ambulance siren split the air.

Hurry, hurry, she silently urged. *Please, dear God, don't let him die.*

Noah rushed to her side. He placed his hands over hers on his brother's leg. "The medics are here."

Two paramedics knelt down beside Carter, nudging her aside. She watched helplessly as they checked his vitals, dressed his wound, stuck an IV in his arm. With Noah's help, the medics moved Carter onto a gurney. She scrambled to her feet and stayed at his side as the men carried him to the back of the ambulance.

"I'm going with you," she told them, and climbed inside the back as Carter was loaded inside. Frosty jumped in with her.

The medic frowned. "Ma'am, that dog can't—"

"It's okay," Noah told the guy. "Let them both go with you." He met her gaze. "When you get to the hospital, call my parents."

She took a shuddering breath as the weight of responsibility and trust being placed on her settled around her like a heavy blanket. "I will. I promise."

He nodded. "I'll be there as soon as I can."

The door of the ambulance shut and the van rolled out of the trucking company parking lot. Through the small windows in the back doors, she saw a handcuffed Miles and his minions being led to a cruiser.

Frosty leaned against her and put his paw on the gurney as if the dog needed to touch his master. She understood.

Carter lay so still. His face was ashen, his lips tinged blue from lack of blood. Her heart lurched.

She gathered Carter's hand in hers. His palm was clammy. She smoothed a hand over his brow as she silently prayed for his survival.

Frosty set his snout on her knee as if he sensed her prayers.

When they reached the hospital, medical personnel whisked Carter away, leaving her and Frosty to quickly follow. Her hand tightened around Frosty's lead as the adrenaline of the day seeped away and tears streamed down her face. Furiously she wiped at them. She had to call the Jamesons. She needed to find a phone.

"Miss?" A nurse—Sue, her name tag read—drew Rachelle's attention. "You're bleeding."

"What?" She looked down at her clothes. Carter's blood stained the fabric. Her breath stalled. "It's not mine."

"Your feet."

Glancing at the floor, she noted a trail of blood leading to her bare feet. In the chaos, she'd forgotten about her feet. "Oh." She dismissed her own need for care with a shake of her head. "I need to make a phone call."

"Let me tend to your feet, then you can make your call." Nurse Sue took her to an exam room. "Are you with the police?" She gave Frosty a wary glance.

"Uh, not me. He is, though," Rachelle said as Frosty stared at them. She reached out and he nuzzled her hand. His vest had splotches of blood embedded in the gold lettering. "His handler was just brought in. I have to call his family."

"You don't want to get an infection in your foot. Let's get this done. I'm not going to lie—this might hurt." Nurse Sue treated her feet for a couple of minor cuts, picking out bits of gravel before bandaging the wounds. Emotionally overwrought, Rachelle hardly felt the nurse's ministrations.

Nurse Sue helped Rachelle into a pair of socks and disposable slippers.

Slipping off the exam table, her feet hit the floor with a sting but she ignored the discomfort. "Is there a phone I can use?"

"This way."

Rachelle shuffled after the woman to the nurses' station. Frosty's nails clicked against the hard floor alongside of Rachelle. He sat with his back to the desk as if keeping watch.

Rachelle picked up the receiver and paused as she realized she didn't know the Jamesons' home number by heart. It was stored in her phone back at the hotel. Despairing she'd fail at the promised task, she frantically dialed the number for information only to be thwarted because the Jamesons' number was unlisted. Frustrated, she called the NYC K-9 Command Unit and asked for Sophie Walters.

"This is Sophie." The woman's voice wavered slightly as if she were upset.

"Sophie, it's Rachelle Clark," Rachelle said.

"I need Alex and Ivy Jameson's home phone number. Carter was—" Her voice broke. She swallowed back the sob threatening to undo her. "I need to tell them where he is."

"We've heard the news." Sophie sniffled. "I can call them."

"No. I promised Noah I would, but I don't have their number. Please, I need to—" A fresh wave of tears coursed down her face, dripping onto the nurses' station counter.

"I understand." Sophie gave her the number.

"Thank you." Rachelle hung up and quickly dialed the Jameson home.

"Hello," Alex answered.

Hearing his voice made her knees buckle. She clung to the counter and mustered every bit of control she possessed to speak coherently. "Alex, Carter's been shot. He's at New York-Presbyterian Queens in Flushing."

There was a moment of silence, then Alex said, "We'll be right there." The line went dead.

Rachelle hung up the phone, feeling raw and desolate. *Now what?* She pushed away from the counter, with Frosty at her side. They wandered down the linoleum hallway until she paused at the door to the hospital's chapel. She entered and sank onto a bench.

Folding her arms over the back of the bench

in front of her, she lowered her head and sobbed. Frosty lay beside her, his head resting on her feet.

She wasn't sure how long she remained there, quietly pleading with God to save Carter. Frosty whined and rose to his feet. Rachelle lifted her head and found Ivy sliding onto the seat beside her.

The knot in her chest twisted. Dread clawed up her throat. "Carter?"

"He's in surgery," Ivy said. "He's going to need a knee replacement, but he'll live."

Rachelle sagged with relief even as more tears fell from her eyes. "I'm so sorry," she whispered.

Ivy's eyes were red-rimmed as she gathered Rachelle in her arms. "This was not your fault."

"But if I hadn't kept investigating—" Her throat constricted with guilt.

"Then you wouldn't be you," Ivy said. "None of us can predict the future. All we can do is trust every moment we have to God."

She leaned away. "I should be the one comforting you." Another wave of guilt crashed over Rachelle. "You were right not to want me in your lives."

Ivy shook her head. "No. I will admit I was wary at first, but we've come to love you, Rachelle. Especially Carter."

Rachelle's breath hitched as pain seared her

heart. "No. Not Carter. He told me there was no room in his life for me."

"Don't give up on him yet," Ivy said. "He may need time to adjust to his feelings, but once he realizes the truth..." She smiled. "I can't wait to see what happens."

Rachelle didn't want to burst Ivy's bubble, but Rachelle had no illusions. There was no future for her with Carter.

A beeping sound, annoying and grating, drew Carter through a groggy haze toward consciousness. The scent of lavender filled his lungs.

He knew that scent.

Rachelle.

Heart leaping with the need to see her, his eyelids fluttered open. Light stung his retinas. After several blinks, his focus adjusted on a water-stained ceiling, sterile beige walls and that incessant beeping to his left. He turned his head to see a monitor gauging his heart rate and blood pressure. An IV bag hung from a stand. His gaze followed the tubing down to his hand, where it disappeared beneath white gauze. He was in the hospital.

The scrape of chair legs on the linoleum floor pierced his ear and echoed inside of his head. He winced.

"Easy now."

He knew that voice.

Rachelle. She really was here.

A cool hand pressed against his forehead, soothing and gentle. He sighed and closed his eyes, his mind wanting to sink back into murkiness. He fought against descending into the bliss of oblivion. He needed to see her dear, lovely face.

"Stay down," she said.

Who was she talking to?

Forcing his eyes to reopen, he turned his head to find her standing beside him, her dark eyes filled with worry even as a smile played on her lips. She wore a pink, feminine top and khaki capris. Her dark hair was clipped back at her nape, the long ends draped over her shoulder. Dark circles under her eyes made his stomach clench. Then Frosty's head appeared over the top of the hospital bed, his dark eyes on Carter's face. Joy at seeing them both spread through him, filling all the empty places.

Where was Ellie? He needed his daughter to complete...

"You're awake," Rachelle said. "We were beginning to think you were going to sleep like Rip van Winkle."

Memory of when he'd last seen Rachelle jackknifed his pulse. A man holding her hostage. The searing pain in his leg. The split second to make a decision that would save Rachelle's life. Her tears.

He jerked, trying to sit up but his head was so foggy and his leg felt heavy, weighted down. "Are you safe?" he questioned. He looked toward the closed door. "Why isn't there a guard? You should be under protection."

If anything happen to her...

She stroked his cheek. "Shhh. Everything is fine. I'm fine." She started to turn away. "I need to tell them you're awake."

He lifted a hand to stop her. "What happened?"

She stepped out of his reach. "Let me get the doctor."

As Rachelle hurried from the room, Frosty put his front paws on the bed next to his head and licked Carter's face.

"I missed you, too, buddy," Carter murmured. He lifted his head and looked at his legs. They were covered with a blanket, but the left knee was propped higher.

The door to the room opened and a man in a white lab coat, a stethoscope around his neck, walked in. He was in his midforties, medium height with jet-black hair and kind hazel eyes.

Behind him, Rachelle slipped back into the room and leaned against the wall, out of the doctor's way.

"Off," Carter instructed Frosty. The dog retreated. "Down." Frosty settled on the floor, his gaze on Carter.

"Well, it's good to see you're alert, Officer Jameson. I'm Dr. Garcia. I've performed your surgery."

"Nice to meet you, I guess," Carter said. "I was shot in the leg."

Dr. Garcia nodded. "Yes. We extracted the bullet from your knee. You lost a lot of blood and you're going to be weak for a little while, but your prognosis is good."

"My knee?" That didn't sound good.

"We reconstructed your left knee. It'll be a while before you'll have full function of your leg. You'll need physical therapy once you're healed enough."

Anxiety twisted in Carter's chest. "Will I be able to walk again?"

"Yes," the doctor said. "However, you may not have full function of your left leg to the same capacity you did prior to your wound."

Carter wasn't sure what to make of the doctor's words. He was just glad that he hadn't lost his leg. But what would that mean for his career with the NYC K-9 Command Unit?

Dr. Garcia made notes on his chart. He noticed Rachelle and smiled. "I'll leave you in good hands."

Rachelle dragged a chair close to the bed. She took his hand in hers. "Your family is waiting to see you. But I just wanted a moment to tell you thank-you. You saved my life." She let out a small, rueful laugh. "Again."

"Miles?"

"Arrested and in custody," she told him. "His men turned on him. They confessed to being a part of Miles's newly formed crew. Apparently, Miles had decided while in prison to take up a new profession as an arms dealer."

"Did he confess to killing my brother?" He held his breath, hoping they'd solved Jordan's murder.

Rachelle shook her head. "No, he denies any connection to Jordan's death. And so far there's been no evidence to put him at the scene of your brother's murder."

Disappointment punched him in the gut. So they were back at square one. But at least Rachelle was safe now.

He thanked God for that huge favor.

"Carter, I—"

A commotion at the door cut Rachelle off as his family pushed through the door.

"Daddy!"

His daughter's sweet voice made his heart leap with joy. Rachelle stepped aside, allowing Ellie to rush the bed. Noah followed and picked Ellie up so that she could lean over to kiss Carter on the forehead. His parents, Zach and Violet and Katie circled the bed.

"Hi, sweet pea. I love you," he told Ellie.

Her bright blue eyes sparkled with tears. "I love you, Daddy. We were all so scared."

He looked at every face in the room. His family. He was a very blessed man. Tears of gratitude gathered in his eyes.

Rachelle slipped behind Noah and Ellie, pausing to say something to Katie and then she walked out the door. Frosty stood and stared after her.

Carter wanted to call her back but Ellie was talking and his head began to pound as pain flowed up his leg. He did his best to listen as each person took a turn to speak to him. He appreciated the love and support even as he gritted his teeth as the ache in his knee intensified.

"Okay, everyone," Ivy said. "We need to let Carter rest."

She urged the others out of the room. His father remained at his side and gathered his hand in his.

His mom came back and sat in the chair Rachelle had vacated. "You're quite the hero."

"Just doing my job," Carter said, his voice cracking.

"Not the way Noah tells it," Alex said. "And you know he's not one to give a ton of praise."

Yes, his stoic brother who didn't like to let his emotions show. If Noah called his actions heroic...

"How long will I be in here?"

"Doc said at least another week," his dad replied.

Carter frowned. "How long have I been here?"

"Three days," his mom said. "And Rachelle has hardly left your side."

"That young lady loves you," his father stated.

Overwhelmed by the thought and the agony rippling through him, Carter turned his head. "I'm tired. My knee is on fire."

His mother patted his hand. "I'll tell the nurse."

But Carter doubted the nurse would bring him anything that could deaden his feelings for Rachelle.

With deep, welling satisfaction, Rachelle sat in her apartment holding a copy of the *NYC Weekly* newspaper and stared at the front page. Her article detailed her ordeal with Miles Landau and the heroic efforts of the NYC K-9 Command Unit, and specifically Officer Carter Jameson and his partner, Frosty, in taking down the arms dealer and keeping this reporter alive.

Her article on the front page! She wanted to dance around the room in joyous abandon. She wanted to shout from the rooftop. She wanted to tell Carter.

Instead she sank farther into the cushions of the couch and grabbed another cookie.

With a sigh borne of heartache, she set the newspaper aside and picked up her computer. She wanted to buy a thank-you present for the Jamesons for all they had done for her. And a gift for Carter and Frosty.

Better to buy something for the dogs. It would be less complicated, have less meaning. No, not less meaning. She owed her life to Frosty, as well as Carter.

She admired and respected the great dogs and men and women of the NYC K-9 Command Unit.

But most especially Carter.

She blew out a frustrated breath. No matter what she did or how much she'd tried over the past three days, she couldn't eradicate Carter from her thoughts. Or the feelings that had flooded her when all the Jamesons had joined her and Carter in his hospital room. There'd been an outpouring of love and support among them and between them.

Leaving her feeling like an outsider.

The familiar sensation had nearly drawn her to her knees right there. Instead, she'd made a quick exit.

She just had to face the knowledge that she'd always be an outsider, no matter where she went or whom she was with.

Maybe some retail therapy would help. The computer was open on a page for dog paraphernalia.

First a little something for Frosty, Scotty and the puppies and the Jamesons, then a little something for herself.

As she scrolled through the various items the cutest thing caught her eye. She smiled.

That's the ticket!

And she placed an order.

SIXTEEN

"Five days," Carter fumed at the doctor reading his chart. "I've been here five days. I want to go home."

And at least twice every day he had picked up the phone to call Rachelle and then talked himself out of dialing her number. He didn't know what to say. He'd never been good at small talk. But it wasn't really the small talk that was the problem. He had a problem telling her of his feelings and broaching the subject of their relationship. He wasn't good at talking about the big stuff.

Dr. Garcia smiled. "You are making great strides. Your blood pressure has normalized, and your blood volume has come up significantly. Alonzo tells me your PT is going well."

Carter snorted. "You mean the torturer torturing me is going well."

Dr. Garcia chuckled. "Yes, physical therapy can be painful."

Carter arched an eyebrow. "That's putting it mildly."

But he was motivated to be able to walk again. He had Frosty to think about. He needed to get back out in the field eventually. Though every time he thought about returning to his beat, Rachelle's words echoed in his head. *Why would you stay in a career that puts you in harm's way? What if something happened to you?*

A bout of panic stole over him. Carter held it in check. The last thing he needed was to go see the department psychologist. Or maybe it was the best thing he could do. Yes, he decided, he would seek help from the department's psych doc.

He didn't want to be a statistic with post-traumatic stress disorder, flinching every time he thought about work.

There was a knock on the door to his hospital room.

Dr. Garcia replaced his chart. "I will come back and check on you later."

He left and in strode Reed Branson and his partner, Jessie. The big female bloodhound trotted at Reed's side.

"Hey, buddy," Reed said. "How are you doing?"

Carter pinched the bridge of his nose. "I've

been better. Tell me something interesting. Fill me in on what's going on at the command unit."

Reed pulled up a chair. "Mostly business as usual. There have been reports of a German shepherd matching Snapper's description seen with a bunch of teens at Coney Island. We're going to check it out." He stroked one of Jessie's ears.

Carter's heart jumped with hope. "Ellie still maintains she saw him in Prospect Park."

"Everyone is keeping an eye out for him," Reed said. "We'll do our part. Jessie's tracking skills are top-notch."

"If we could find Snapper that would be a huge blessing." Carter hated to think they'd never see the dog again. "I wish I wasn't stuck here. Frosty and I would go with you."

"I'd like nothing better," Reed said. "Soooo," he drew out the word. "Rachelle."

Carter glanced at his buddy sharply. A stab of fear hit him in the chest. "What about her?"

"Haven't you heard the good news?"

"What good news?"

"She has a job interview with the *New York Times*."

Surprise and pleasure erupted inside Carter's chest, melting the fear away. "That's great." He wondered why his parents and his brothers hadn't mentioned it. Probably because every time they brought Rachelle up, he shut them down. He sighed. "I'm so proud of her."

"Did you read her article about you?"

Carter glanced at the stack of *NYC Weekly* newspapers on the bed tray. He still couldn't believe she mentioned him, calling him a hero and touting his and Frosty's finesse. His heart swelled with affection when he read and reread the articles she'd written. And every time, he tamped the tender emotion back into the box of things he'd rather not deal with.

"She's got a thing for you, you know." Reed waggled his eyebrows.

"Yeah, that's what everybody keeps saying. But I don't believe it." More like he didn't want to believe it. Because if she cared for him, she'd only end up hurt in the end, because he couldn't…

"Dude, she would hardly leave your side. After you were shot, she was the one who ran to you and put her hand over the wound. She rode in the ambulance with you and Frosty. And she stayed here until you woke up."

"I understand she needed to make sure I was okay, because I saved her life. And then she left." Without saying goodbye or anything. He'd been surprised by the hurt that had burrowed in deep after her abrupt departure.

"Did you ask her to stay?"

"She didn't give me a chance."

Reed tucked in his chin. "There's this thing called a phone. You could call her and ask her to come back."

Carter shook his head. "I would only interrupt her life. Complicate it. I don't want to mess up what she has going for herself."

Reed shook his head. "I never thought you'd be one to hide from the truth."

Carter stared. "What do you mean, hide from the truth? I'm not hiding from anything."

Reed rubbed his chin. "Maybe not, but maybe you are hiding from your own truth."

His friend's words dug deep inside of Carter, breaking loose something he'd tried so hard to ignore, to deny. Something he'd been hiding. He did love Rachelle.

But the truth was he couldn't do anything about it. He just couldn't. He wasn't brave enough, no matter what Rachelle had written about him.

Two days later, Carter was finally home. At least to his parents' apartment. He wouldn't be able to take the stairs to his, Ellie's and Noah's apartment quite yet. His dad had built a wheelchair ramp so that they could wheel him through the front door of their place.

A chorus of "Welcome home" erupted and

echoed throughout the house and inside his heart. There was a Welcome Home banner stretched across the wood beam separating the dining room from the living room. There was a cake on the table.

He searched for Rachelle but she wasn't there. Disappointment lay heavy on his heart even as he smiled and opened his arms for Ellie to climb up onto his lap.

"Hey, munchkin."

"Welcome home, Daddy. We love you."

His heart swelled with love for his daughter and those gathered around.

There was a scratch at the back door.

His mother hurried over and opened the door. Frosty, Scotty and Eddie rushed in, followed by the growing bundles of fur that were the puppies. Honestly, they had doubled in size since he'd last seen them. Frosty ran to the side of the wheelchair and propped his paws up on the arm of the wheelchair. Carter leaned over and nuzzled the dog. Frosty licked his face. Everyone laughed.

Carter drew back and looked at Frosty. "What is he wearing?"

Frosty had a black T-shirt with white lettering that read, "I'm the big dog, don't mess with me." Scotty had on a T-shirt that read, "I'm the other big dog, don't mess with me."

Ellie slipped off his lap and picked up one of the puppies. "Rachelle sent them."

Ivy picked up the other. "Aren't they adorable?" Ivy asked.

Each pup had on a navy T-shirt that had gold lettering that read, "K-9 In-Training."

He looked at the puppies then back at Frosty. He laughed. "That is so thoughtful and funny and so Rachelle."

His heart ached with missing her.

"Somebody get this man some cake," his father said.

Later, after the party, Carter sat with Noah and Zach in the living room while Ellie helped his mom clean up in the kitchen and his dad was out back with the dogs.

"We invited Rachelle," Noah stated.

"Let me guess," Carter said. "She declined." His stomach clenched. He couldn't blame her.

Noah's jaw tightened. "She did. Citing she had to work. But really I think she was being stubborn."

"Stubborn?"

"Yes, just like you're being," Noah chastised.

"I don't know what you're talking about."

Zach punched Carter on the shoulder. "That woman loves you—we all know it."

Noah sat on the coffee table in front of Carter and placed his elbows on his knees, steepling his fingers, looking like he was settling in for a lecture. "Brother, you know we love you. And so you have to understand this comes with love."

Uh-oh. Noah was using the *L* word—this was pretty serious.

Zach nodded. "You're our brother. We want to see you happy."

"Like you're happy?" Carter suggested.

Zach grinned. "Exactly. I am blissfully happy. Violet is the best thing in my life."

Carter looked at Noah. "Don't tell me you believe in love."

"Not for myself, but I can recognize it when I see it. You love Rachelle and she loves you. And you're both being stubborn and idiotic." He ran a hand through his hair. "All I'm saying is, you have a chance at something wonderful with a wonderful woman. Don't blow it."

Carter's heart thumped against his rib cage. "Her career is taking off. She's interviewing with the *New York Times*. I would only hold her back."

Zach scoffed. "It's not like she moved away. She can have her dream job and be with you and Ellie."

"But what if her career takes her somewhere else?" He knew he was grasping for an excuse not to accept their words.

Zach made a choking noise. "What's bigger than the *New York Times*?"

Noah narrowed his gaze on Carter. "You're afraid." He nodded his head, satisfied with his assessment. "Yeah, that's it. Carter is afraid of love."

Carter gripped the handrails of the wheelchair.

"No. I loved Helen. I love Ellie."

Zach put his hand over Carter's. "Brother, what's holding you back?"

Carter slipped his hand out from under Zach's and grabbed the wheels and pushed but the wheels wouldn't budge. He wanted to get away from them, get away from this line of questioning. But the brakes were on the wheelchair. Giving up on rolling away, he tried to push himself to his good foot but his brothers pushed him back down into the chair.

"You're not going anywhere until you face this," Noah said in his most commanding tone.

Trapped, Carter spit out, "Fine. I'm afraid." The confession burst from him. "I'm afraid of losing her. I'm afraid of loving and going through the kind of pain I had when Helen died."

Zach nodded. "I understand. I really do. When Violet was being threatened, I knew my life would end if something happened to her."

"But you saved her. You protected her," Carter said.

"Just like you did for Rachelle," Noah pointed out. "Just as you would in the future."

"But what if something happens that I can't control?" Carter's voice broke. He hadn't been able to protect or save his wife. Her death had been out of his control.

Zach and Noah looked at each other. Then back at Carter.

"You know what Mom says," Noah stated.

"Only God's in control," Zach finished.

Carter had heard his mother and others say this his whole life. But accepting the words took faith and he wasn't sure he had enough faith for a second time.

He felt a hand on his shoulder and looked up at his mother. Beside her, Ellie clutched her hand. "Son, we love you. We all love you and we know Helen would want you to be happy."

His dad had said the same thing. But was it true?

Ellie climbed up into his lap and took his face between her little hands and stared into his eyes. "Daddy, do you love Rachelle?"

He could never lie to his child. Emotion swelled in his throat. He swallowed convulsively before he could speak. "Yes, honey, I do."

The admission allowed peace to flow through him. No more hiding from the truth.

A beaming grin broke out on his daughter's face and she let out a loud whoop before she slipped her arms around his neck and hugged him.

"I do, too," Ellie whispered into his ear. He could feel her wet tears on his neck.

The back door opened and his father walked in, along with five curious dogs.

Frosty sat next to him and whined; clearly the dog sensed that Carter was upset. Carter patted Frosty reassuringly.

"What's going on in here?" Alex demanded.

Noah stood up and clapped his dad on the back. "I'll let them explain. I need to get back to the command center." He whistled for Scotty, who followed at his heels as Noah strode out the door.

Zach rose, and his dog, Eddie, a floppy-eared beagle, hurried to his side. "Violet's upstairs with Katie. I'm going to go see the ladies." As he and Eddie passed by Carter, Zach squeezed his shoulder. "Proud of you, man."

While Ivy filled in Alex, the puppies barked and raced around the room, a cute distraction.

"Daddy?"

Carter looked into his daughter's serious gaze. "Yes, sweet pea?"

"Don't you think we ought to go tell Rachelle?"

He chuckled. Leave it to his daughter to point out the obvious. "Yes, I think we should."

Ivy clapped her hands. "We'll drive you."

"Now?" Carter questioned with a laugh.

"No time like the present," Alex interjected, grabbing the back of the wheelchair and unlocking the wheels.

"Can the dogs come, too?" Ellie asked as she climbed off her father's lap.

"Sure, why not?" Carter said. "Let's make this a family affair."

They loaded him up into the wheelchair-accessible van that his father had rented.

"Do you mind if we stop at a store on the way?" Carter asked.

Ivy beamed at him. "Flowers! Good thinking, son."

That hadn't occurred to him. But flowers would be good, too.

But he had something else in mind, as well.

Rachelle completed the finishing touches on the article about the zoos in the five boroughs, then hit Submit, and off the document went to her editor at *NYC Weekly*.

She hoped and prayed at some point she'd be able to write a story about how the NYC K-9 Command Unit finally closed the case on

Jordan Jameson's death and captured the villain who'd taken their chief, friend and family member's life.

Maybe even for the *New York Times* if they called her back for a second interview. She thought the first one went well. She'd had other news sources calling, showing interest, but she quickly realized they only wanted insider information on the K-9 Unit and the Jameson family specifically. She shut down those inquires fast and hard.

A knock at the door startled her. She wasn't expecting anyone. She opened the door to find Carter sitting in a wheelchair, a brown paper bag in his lap and a bouquet of flowers in his hand. Ellie stood on one side of him, her sweet little face beaming, and Frosty on the other side of Carter while Ivy and Alex stood behind him, each holding a puppy.

The dogs were wearing the T-shirts she'd sent them. Her heart raced. Happiness to see the Jamesons had her pulse tripping over itself. "This is an unexpected surprise."

Frosty trotted in and sniffed around.

"May we come in?" Carter asked.

Where were her manners? "Of course, please."

She stood back. Alex handed off his pup to Ivy, then pushed Carter into the middle of the living room. Ellie rushed forward to wrap her arms around Rachelle.

Heart thumping, Rachelle bent and picked her up in a tight hug. Fighting back tears, she set Ellie down as Alex gave Rachelle a quick hug before taking Ellie by the hand and backing out of the apartment to stand next to his wife in the doorway.

"We'll be out here in the hall," Ivy said, and she grabbed the door handle and shut the door.

Surprised and a bit wary, Rachelle turned to Carter. "I don't understand? Why are they not coming in?"

For a long moment, Carter just stared at her. There was a look in his eyes that made her both nervous and thrilled at the same time.

He thrust out the bouquet of gerbera daisies. "These are for you. I didn't know what kind of flower you like. But these were the brightest and prettiest. Ellie thought that you would like them."

She took the flowers and hugged them to her chest. "I love them. Gerbera daisies are actually one of my favorite flowers. And you're right, so vivid. All the pinks and oranges and yellows. They can brighten any gloomy day."

Carter frowned. "Are you having a gloomy day?"

She didn't want to tell him she'd been having many gloomy days lately. Ever since he'd been shot.

"It's my fault," he said.

"What? What are you talking about?"

"Your gloomy days," he said as if he'd somehow read her thoughts. "I'm sorry, Rachelle. I have to confess something to you."

The wariness turned to dread. "Should I be sitting down?"

He gave her a wry smile. "No, this isn't anything earth-shattering. I'm sure it's something you already suspect."

Wanting to stall whatever he had to tell her, she moved into the kitchen to grab a vase. Her hands shook as she filled the vase with water and put the flowers in and carried the vase to the dining room table. Finally, she bolstered her courage and turned around. "Okay. Tell me."

Carter licked his lips. He looked at the bag he was holding. He held the bag out to her. "Oh, this is for you, too."

Curious what he'd bring her in a brown paper bag, she took the bag and peeked inside. Surprised pleasure spread through her as she lifted out the almond-based ice cream.

"How did you know?"

"You didn't think I noticed that you don't drink or eat dairy. But, Rachelle, I notice everything about you." His voice turned husky with emotion. "I see you for who you are. A kind, compassionate and loving woman."

Tears gathered in her eyes as she stared at him. "This is the sweetest thing anyone has ever done for me."

His eyebrows rose. "Aw, Rachelle. That breaks my heart to hear that giving you ice cream is the nicest thing anybody's ever done. If you let me, I will do so much more for you, for us."

She blinked as tears fell down her cheek. "Carter, what are you saying?"

"I'm saying I've been afraid. Too afraid to allow my heart to open up to anyone except my family. I realize that isolating myself wasn't being fair to Ellie or to the memory of Helen."

Rachelle sucked in a breath. "You still love your wife."

"Yes," he said. "I always will. But I know Helen would want me to make room in my heart for more love. She would want me to be happy." He held out his hand. "You make me happy, Rachelle."

She couldn't believe what she was hearing. Words she'd longed to hear her whole life.

Carter let his hand rest back on the wheel-chair arm. "I would understand if you don't feel the same. But I just need you to know that I love you."

Her feet felt rooted to the spot. All the love she felt for him welled up until her throat closed and she felt like she would pass out from the lack of oxygen. A gentle nudge at her knees drew her attention away from Carter. Frosty pushed her gently toward his partner. It was all the encouragement she needed.

She closed the distance between her and Carter and went down on her knees next to his wheelchair. Setting the ice cream aside, she looked at him with all the love and joy she possessed. "I love you, too, Carter."

He breathed out a breath and smiled as he framed her face with his hands and leaned in to kiss her. His lips molded exquisitely against hers.

For a long moment, she lost herself in the sensations rocketing over her and through her, heart beating with joy and love.

Frosty let out a single bark.

The tiniest squeak of the front door alerted her before there was an eruption of clapping and whooping as Ellie, Ivy, Alex and the puppies charged inside the apartment.

Reluctantly, Rachelle drew away from Carter with a bemused smile.

He stared at his family. "Were you listening at the door?"

Alex pointed to Ivy. She shrugged, totally unrepentant.

"Does this mean you're going to get married?" Ellie asked as she squeezed in between Rachelle and Carter, wrapping an arm around each of them.

Rachelle met Carter's gaze, her breath caught in her lungs as she waited for his response.

"If she'll have me," he said.

"Yes. Yes, a thousand times over," she answered.

Ivy clapped her hands again. "Another wedding. I'm so excited."

"We're going to have to wait, though," Carter said. "I want to be able to stand at the altar. Without crutches."

Remembering something Katie had said about wishing she and Jordan had had more time to get to know each other, Rachelle nodded. "I don't mind waiting. It'll give us an opportunity to get to know each other better without all the drama and danger."

Carter frowned. "It won't be that long. I'll double my PT regimen and do whatever I can. Maybe in a month or two?"

"That's perfect," Ivy said, pulling Rachelle to

her feet for a hug. "We'll have to go dress shopping right away."

Overwhelmed with joy, Rachelle felt like she was going to burst.

Carter captured her hand. "You won't just be marrying me," he said, his gaze intent and serious. "You will be joining our family, which includes the NYC K-9 Command Unit."

She touched his cheek. "I couldn't ask for more."

Carter turned his head and kissed the palm of her hand.

* * * * *

If you enjoyed Seeking the Truth,
look for Reed Branson's story,
Trail of Danger,
coming up next, and the rest of the
True Blue K-9 Unit series from
Love Inspired Suspense.

True Blue K-9 Unit:
These police officers fight for justice
with the help of their brave canine partners

Dear Reader,

I hope you've enjoyed this story of Officer Carter Jameson and his partner, Frosty. Together, they made a dynamic team perfectly suited to protect and fall in love with reporter Rachelle Clark. Carter and Rachelle both had issues from their past they had to overcome before they could let down the walls around their hearts.

Writing this story against the backdrop of New York City was a treat. I lived on the Upper West Side of Manhattan as a young adult and the experience was one I treasure. Combining my love of the city with K-9 dogs and handlers was a special joy for me. Plus, working with such a wonderful group of authors and editors is always a blessing.

The next book in the series, *Trail of Danger* by Valerie Hansen, will be released September 2019—you won't want to miss it.

You'll be able to find the whole continuity series on www.harlequin.com.

Blessings,

Get 4 FREE REWARDS!

We'll send you 2 FREE Books plus 2 FREE Mystery Gifts.

Love Inspired® books feature contemporary inspirational romances with Christian characters facing the challenges of life and love.

FREE Value Over **$20**

YES! Please send me 2 FREE Love Inspired® Romance novels and my 2 FREE mystery gifts (gifts are worth about $10 retail). After receiving them, if I don't wish to receive any more books, I can return the shipping statement marked "cancel." If I don't cancel, I will receive 6 brand-new novels every month and be billed just $5.24 for the regular-print edition or $5.99 each for the larger-print edition in the U.S., or $5.74 each for the regular-print edition or $6.24 each for the larger-print edition in Canada. That's a savings of at least 13% off the cover price. It's quite a bargain! Shipping and handling is just 50¢ per book in the U.S. and $1.25 per book in Canada.* I understand that accepting the 2 free books and gifts places me under no obligation to buy anything. I can always return a shipment and cancel at any time. The free books and gifts are mine to keep no matter what I decide.

Choose one: ☐ **Love Inspired® Romance Regular-Print** (105/305 IDN GNWC)   ☐ **Love Inspired® Romance Larger-Print** (122/322 IDN GNWC)

Name (please print)

Address   Apt. #

City   State/Province   Zip/Postal Code

Mail to the **Reader Service:**
IN U.S.A.: P.O. Box 1341, Buffalo, NY 14240-8531
IN CANADA: P.O. Box 603, Fort Erie, Ontario L2A 5X3

Want to try 2 free books from another series? Call 1-800-873-8635 or visit www.ReaderService.com.

Get 4 FREE REWARDS!

We'll send you 2 FREE Books plus 2 FREE Mystery Gifts.

Harlequin® Heartwarming™ Larger-Print books feature traditional values of home, family, community and—most of all—love.

FREE
Value Over
$20

THE FORTUNES OF TEXAS COLLECTION!

18 FREE BOOKS in all!

Treat yourself to the rich legacy of the Fortune and Mendoza clans in this remarkable 50-book collection. This collection is packed with cowboys, tycoons and Texas-sized romances!

YES! Please send me **The Fortunes of Texas Collection** in Larger Print. This collection begins with 3 FREE books and 2 FREE gifts in the first shipment. Along with my 3 free books, I'll also get the next 4 books from The Fortunes of Texas Collection, in LARGER PRINT, which I may either return and owe nothing, or keep for the low price of $5.24 U.S./$5.89 CDN each plus $2.99 for shipping and handling per shipment*. If I decide to continue, about once a month for 8 months I will get 6 or 7 more books but will only need to pay for 4. That means 2 or 3 books in every shipment will be FREE! If I decide to keep the entire collection, I'll have paid for only 32 books because 18 books are FREE! I understand that accepting the 3 free books and gifts places me under no obligation to buy anything. I can always return a shipment and cancel at any time. My free books and gifts are mine to keep no matter what I decide.

☐ 269 HCN 4622   ☐ 469 HCN 4622

Name (please print)

Address   Apt. #

City   State/Province   Zip/Postal Code

Mail to the **Reader Service:**
IN U.S.A.: P.O. Box 1341, Buffalo, N.Y. 14240-8531
IN CANADA: P.O. Box 603, Fort Erie, Ontario L2A 5X3

COMING NEXT MONTH FROM
Love Inspired® Suspense

Available September 3, 2019

TRAIL OF DANGER
True Blue K-9 Unit • by Valerie Hansen
When Abigail Jones wakes up injured from an attack she doesn't remember, she knows someone's after her, but she doesn't know *why*. Now only the man who rescued her, Officer Reed Branson, and his K-9 partner can keep her safe while she regains her memory.

DANGEROUS RELATIONS
The Baby Protectors • by Carol J. Post
When her sister is killed, Shelby Adair's determined to keep her young niece away from the father's shady family—especially since she's convinced they were behind the murder. But after the killer attempts to kidnap little Chloe, can Shelby trust the child's uncle, Ryan McConnell, with their lives?

DEADLY EVIDENCE
Mount Shasta Secrets • by Elizabeth Goddard
FBI agent Tori Peterson intends to find her sister's murderer, even if it makes her a target. But that means returning home and working with the lead detective—her ex-boyfriend, Ryan Bradley. With someone willing to kill to keep the truth hidden, can Tori and Ryan survive the investigation?

UNDERCOVER TWIN
Twins Separated at Birth • by Heather Woodhaven
Audrey Clark never knew she was a twin—until she stumbled onto a covert operation. Now with her FBI agent sister in critical condition, Audrey's the only one who can complete the mission. But with danger around every corner, can she avoid falling for her pretend husband, FBI agent Lee Benson?

RECOVERED SECRETS
by Jessica R. Patch
Two years ago, a woman with amnesia washed up on the banks of search-and-rescue director Hollis Montgomery's small Mississippi town. The woman he calls Grace still has no idea who she really is, but they finally have a clue: someone wants her dead.

FATAL MEMORIES
by Tanya Stowe
It's DEA agent Dylan Murphy's job to take down a drug ring, including border patrol officer Jocelyn Walker's brother. But he's not sure whether Jocelyn is innocent...and without her memory, neither is she. Now it's Dylan's job to protect her from the gang dead set on silencing her for good.

LOOK FOR THESE AND OTHER LOVE INSPIRED BOOKS WHEREVER BOOKS ARE SOLD, INCLUDING MOST BOOKSTORES, SUPERMARKETS, DISCOUNT STORES AND DRUGSTORES.

LISCNM0819